Regicide

T0154665

Also by Nicholas Royle

Novels
Counterparts
Saxophone Dreams
The Matter of the Heart
The Director's Cut
Antwerp

Novellas
The Appetite
The Enigma of Departure

Short stories
Mortality

Anthologies (as editor)
Darklands
Darklands 2
A Book of Two Halves
The Tiger Garden: A Book of Writers' Dreams
The Time Out Book of New York Short Stories
The Ex Files: New Stories About Old Flames
The Agony & the Ecstasy: New Writing for the World Cup
Neonlit: Time Out Book of New Writing
The Time Out Book of Paris Short Stories
Neonlit: Time Out Book of New Writing Volume 2
The Time Out Book of London Short Stories Volume 2
Dreams Never End
'68: New Stories From Children of the Revolution
The Best British Short Stories 2011

Regicide

Nicholas Royle

SOLARIS

First published 2011 by Solaris
an imprint of Rebellion Publishing Ltd,
Riverside House, Osney Mead,
Oxford, OX1 0ES, UK

www.solarisbooks.com

ISBN: 978-1-907992-00-1

10 9 8 7 6 5 4 3 2 1

A CIP catalogue record for this book is available from the
British Library.

Designed & typeset by Rebellion Publishing

Printed in the US

To the memory of the Passage, 1978-1983

Part One

'There are few things impossible in themselves; it is the application required, rather than the means to make them succeed, that we lack.'

La Rochefoucauld, *Maximes*

Chapter One

THIS IS WHAT happened *before* I found the map.

I went out with Annie Risk. I'd met her only two days earlier at Jaz's party. We went out to a pub and for something to eat in the West End, and then afterwards I was leading the way back to her hotel because I thought I knew where I was going. I should have done, having worked as a cycle courier in a former life. Still, there would always be one or two areas where my sense of direction would fail me. Grey areas between districts, where the streets appeared indistinguishable from each other.

Annie Risk didn't know this part of London at all, so she was relying on me. It was only sensible, although she clearly didn't like giving up responsibility, especially to a man. But by the end of the evening I think she'd decided I was probably all right. She could trust me this far. In any case, now that I'd lost my way, we were equals again.

One street turned into another at a right angle. None of them appeared to be named and the Georgian terraces that lined them looked identical. The windows were dark, the doors locked tight. The air was warm. We turned right and right again, then went straight on and turned right once more.

I sensed Annie watching me as I pushed my nose forward into the sticky night haze of petrol fumes and fast food. She must have thought I was trying to sniff our way out. I was. My sense of smell is renowned. Or it should be. I wondered what she made of my appearance. I had long hair which had been dyed black so many times it was beginning to spoil. My face is big and stupid – open and kind, an old girlfriend had told me; I'd like to believe it – and by late evening it's usually dark with stubble. My eyes are grey and they don't always manage to hold your gaze. Although it depends who you are, I suppose. At the time I had this beaten old white leather jacket which I loved and wore always. With it that evening, if my memory is reliable, I was wearing a baggy white cotton shirt and tight black jeans. Jaz often told me the jeans made me look ridiculous; other people just said they were retro. In any case, they emphasised the thinness of my legs, which for one so tall – I'm over six foot – did make me look kind of odd. My cowboy boots – worn outside the jeans – were black with a white butterfly motif on the back. Because of the pack of Camels I kept down the left one I walked with a slight limp.

I don't know, I liked the way I looked, or I'd grown used to it and felt pretty comfortable about it. It had been a long time since I'd had to worry about what someone else might think.

I kept looking around for landmarks. But there weren't any and if the doors had numbers, I couldn't bloody well see them.

'It's around here some place,' I said, peering into the gloom for a way out of the seemingly endless maze. A pulse in my temple had begun to irritate me and I thought I might be getting a headache. The night air was close and thick. But the evening had filled me with hope and I was determined not to let things get to me. These streets couldn't go on forever. We'd find Annie's hotel. I hoped she wouldn't think me foolish for leading her into this warren and not being able to find the way out.

'It must be quite an expensive hotel,' I said. The area we were in – south of Euston Road, east of Paddington, on the edge of Marylebone – was not exactly cheap.

'Actually no,' she said. 'Not for me anyway. It's run by a friend of a friend of mine's dad and I get a special rate. It's where I always stay now when I come to London.'

The distance from one streetlamp to the next remained constant. The windows on all sides were dark, many of them shuttered.

'How often do you come down, then?' I asked her as I glanced across the street.

'The last time must have been two, three years ago.'

The pulse in my head throbbed. I wondered if I'd had too much to drink. 'It's not exactly a regular thing then?' I said.

She lived in Manchester in her own flat and earned her living as a graphic designer. Already, from the sparse details she'd given me, I'd pieced together a picture of her flat. Tucked away in a row of terraces like the ones filing past us now, it was small and warm. She liked cushions and hanging things – rugs on the wall and curtains in doorways – and somewhere there would be a kitten drowsing. In contrast to all of this would be her computer, occupying pride of

place on the small desk by the window. I imagined
her sitting there early in the morning perhaps, still in
her dressing gown, the cat purring in her lap, as she
clicked and double-clicked, pulling the design on the
screen one way and squeezing it then changing her
mind and altering the whole thing.

At Jaz's party I'd been struck by her right away.
We'd chatted a bit and after several beers I was
relaxed enough to ask if I could see her again. She'd
said no. But it was in my nature not to give in, even
if I sensed complete futility. *Anything's possible* had
always been my motto, though with women this was
more an article of faith than the result of experience.

Annie had said it wasn't a good idea because she
would be going back to Manchester, and in any case
she didn't want to complicate her life.

She was about five foot five with black hair, dark
eyes of indeterminate colour, a loose top, a baggy
dark grey and green cotton skirt with tassels and
lace-up leather boots. The more we talked, the less
I allowed myself to be distracted and the more I felt
my slightly drunken smile relaxing into a stupid grin.

She'd finally given in to my request in spite of her
resolve. Perhaps she saw something in me she liked.
We could have some fun before she went back, she
might have been thinking.

'Just go for a drink,' she said.

'Maybe something to eat as well,' I pushed.

'OK, but then I'm going back to my hotel and
back to Manchester.'

I raised my hands in innocence.

We met in town, just off Cambridge Circus. I'd
walked down from the Caledonian Road after
locking up the shop. She was wearing a cut-off red
denim jacket and the same tasselled skirt as at the

party. Her dark hair was drawn back in a ponytail; a few strands escaped and fell in front of her ears.

I stopped staring and we stepped into the Cambridge for a drink. We stayed for over an hour and when we came out Annie's hair was loose. She was no longer making a clear effort to remain beyond my reach, but I hung back nevertheless.

Usually, when I knew someone only from afar and then spent time with them in close company I saw through the daunting exterior to the younger, more vulnerable person underneath. Some men revealed themselves as boys and in my eyes would never grow up again. Annie showed signs of the girl she had been but that was all they were – signs and clues to the woman she had become. She laughed a lot after we'd had a couple of drinks and though her words of warning about going back to Manchester free of complications rang clearly in my head, I began to feel that more might be possible.

We had some pasta in a scruffy little Italian, the Centrale, and shared a bottle of wine. Annie's eyes sparkled. Still I didn't push it.

'I'll walk you to your hotel,' I suggested as we hit the sultry pavement again.

She fluffed her hair with both hands. 'I could get a cab.'

'It's a lovely night,' I said, reaching into my left boot for my cigarettes. I cupped my hand around my lighter. She told me the address of the hotel and I said confidently, 'I know where that is. No problem.' We walked through Soho. I noticed people glancing at us. We looked good together. I said to her, 'The world is full of all sorts of possibilities and you've got to make the most of them, or what's the point?'

'Yeah, right,' she said.

I had thought I was happy being single but now I was excited. As I sneaked sidelong glances I saw her lips constantly breaking into a smile. *No complications*, she'd said. Yeah, right.

'How long have you lived in London?' she asked me.

'Nine years,' I told her. 'But it was working as a courier that helped me find my way around. That's when I met Jaz.'

We crossed Oxford Street and turned left towards Regent Street.

'It's warm, isn't it?'

Annie nodded. 'Do you know the way?' she double-checked.

'Oh yes.'

The deeper into the maze we penetrated the more hopeless our chances seemed to become of finding the hotel, at least before its front door was shut for the night. And yet, I thought, the further we walked the nearer we were to eventually hitting a street I recognised.

'You're very optimistic,' she said.

'I've always thought you can influence the outcome by the way you think,' I said, while she looked unconvinced. 'I know these streets...' I went on, and her look changed to one of incredulity. 'I mean I don't know this actual street but I can picture the area on the map and it's impossible to get lost. As long as we keep walking, sooner or later we'll reach a familiar street.'

'They all look familiar to me,' she said. 'Familiar to each other.'

I had to admit she was right, and for a moment I imagined we'd entered another world in which quiet city streets could multiply. It was that kind of evening. It felt weird. The only limits seemed to be those of my imagination.

IT WAS ONLY when we heard the telephone ringing in the next street that we realised how strangely quiet it had been up until then. Not only were the streets we were walking through devoid of traffic, but there was no distant murmur of cars heading west on the Marylebone Road. There were no sirens wailing beyond Baker Street, no Tube trains rumbling underneath our feet, there was no drunken abuse being hurled from pub doorways. There weren't any pubs.

So we both heard the phone before we reached the street. The ringing got louder as we approached the house it was coming from: a house with dark windows just like those on either side, with nothing special about it apart from this insistent ringing.

I looked at Annie and she smiled nervously. I raised my eyebrows and we carried on past without stopping.

'I wonder who's ringing,' she said as we turned into the next street.

I shrugged my shoulders. 'It must be important to keep ringing for so long and this late.' The sound was barely audible now and I realised that was because other noises had intruded. I could plainly hear the faint hum of passing traffic and the light step of pedestrians coming from the end of the street.

We turned right and a hundred yards later stumbled blinking into Marylebone High Street. Looking at each other, we said nothing. I just took a cigarette from the pack squeezed down my boot and lit up.

'It's straightforward now,' I said, loping into my stride and casting an eye back for Annie. She seemed to be walking closer to me, whereas I had expected she might back off now we were in more familiar surroundings. I slowed down fractionally to allow her to catch up. If she did decide to see me, would I always be as thoughtful? Was that what she was thinking?

We walked on.

'This is it,' I said, taking a step back from the building and looking up at the full height of it. 'It doesn't exactly leap out at you, does it?'

There was no hotel sign, just a polished brass plaque bearing the number 23. Something about it disturbed me and the pulse in my head returned. I made a mental note to drink several glasses of water before going to bed. 'Why so low key?' I asked, nodding towards the hotel.

Annie shrugged. 'They don't need to try? I don't know.'

For a few moments we both stood there awkwardly, a yard apart in front of the hotel.

'Well, thank you,' I began as I bent down to kiss her on the cheek. But I didn't finish because she turned her face towards mine and met my mouth with hers. She allowed the tiniest amount of give and I could sense the hardness of her teeth behind the softness of her lips. I felt an instant, euphoric pleasure.

Annie pulled away and looked down. Apart from feeling I ought to apologise for the taste of my cigarettes, I didn't know what to say or do.

Annie was muttering something about going in before they shut the door. Her cheeks were flushed.

'Thanks for a lovely evening,' she said as she made for the doors, probably hoping I wouldn't ask the question I wanted to ask: could I see her again? She looked back. I'd started to look away and my hair had fallen forward to curtain my face, so she almost certainly couldn't make out my expression.

I watched through the glass in the door until she'd collected her key and been swallowed by the ornate, gilt-decorated lift, then threw my head back and took in a deep breath from the stifling night. I made off down the street like a child wading through the shallows at the seashore. My mind was swimming with pictures of Annie's upturned face, thoughts about seeing her again and the smells and sensations of her hair brushing my cheeks as we kissed. I found myself yearning for more. There was no excitement the equal of this. Anything really was possible now. I turned left, and right at the bottom of the street, then left again, heading east.

Because my head was full of Annie Risk it took me a while to realise I was locked back into the maze of streets it had taken us so long to negotiate before. It was the silence that made me realise it and, once again, only when I heard the faint ringing of a telephone. Something made me believe that it was not only the same telephone, but that it had been ringing non-stop since we'd passed it on the way to the hotel.

Soon I was in the very same street and approaching the house. The ringing grew louder. I looked around: the street was empty, all the windows plunged into dark reflection. The thick air enveloped me like the still waters of a deep pool. The telephone continued to ring.

I reached into my boot for a cigarette and spun the wheel on my lighter.

The telephone rang.

I took a deep drag and dropped the cigarette without bothering to grind it with my boot heel.

Afterwards I couldn't fully account for what I did next except by restating the fact that it was a weird evening. Getting lost in streets I thought I knew. Also, I was high on a cocktail of drink, cigarettes, arousal, imagination and Annie Risk. It felt as if the universe were spinning around me. I felt a compulsion and I didn't question it. I just went ahead and did it.

Within moments I had climbed the four steps and tried the door, only to find it locked. I took off my jacket and bunched it up against a small square pane in the window. Delivering one swift punch to the jacket I broke the glass which seemed to melt rather than shatter and flow into the interior gloom.

The telephone was still ringing.

I reached an arm through the hole and fiddled with the catch until it sprang open. The window opened easily after that and I jumped into the room. For one sickening airborne instant I feared the floor would give way under my feet, but it was solid.

I crouched and looked around. The ringing seemed to be coming from a room deeper inside the house. Slipping into my jacket I stepped as lightly as possible to the door, my way lit by the glow of streetlamps. In the hallway, illuminated by a faint glimmer from the half-moon of stained glass above the door, I orientated myself. The ringing was coming from the dark end of the hall. My breathing had become shallow. It was not only that I was frightened by the possibility of disturbing the owner of the house, I was still gripped by the feeling that this wasn't an ordinary evening. I was buzzing. I had to answer the phone. It was important.

At the end of the hall were two doors.

I tried them both. The telephone was behind the second.

I saw it from the doorway. Black and lobster-like it sat hunched on a small wooden table draped with a white sheet which looked as if it had been daubed with black ink.

It was still ringing; now, of course, louder than ever.

The thick carpet sucked at my feet as I started to cross the room and I worried I might lose a boot. The air in the room smelt musty and old, as if by opening the door I had broken the seal on a long-kept secret. Perhaps the phone had always been ringing. Air swirled past me as I used my arms like a swimmer to move forward.

I hesitated for a moment as I stood over the little table. What if the phone went dead just before I picked it up? I almost hoped it would.

I lifted the receiver and the ringing stopped. The Bakelite felt clammy in my hand as I raised it to my ear. On the edge of hysteria a woman's voice just had the chance to utter these words – 'Carl! Help! Come quickly, Carl! Please!' – before the connection was severed.

As I stood there in the darkness and the line buzzed, I became more and more frightened.

I didn't tell you my name, did I? That was deliberate. As you'll have guessed, my name is Carl.

Chapter Two

THE FOLLOWING MORNING I went back to the area in which Annie Risk and I had got lost. It was a Sunday so I didn't have to worry about the shop.

I drove around for half an hour, but it was daylight and I could read all the street names and there were numbers on most of the doors. If I did drive down the street where I'd broken into the house to answer the phone, I was unable to recognise it. Certainly I didn't see any broken windows.

Confused, I went back home and rang Jaz. I asked if he was busy and could I come around for a bit.

'Yeah, I'm busy,' he said. 'But come round anyway, you old bastard.'

I drove down through Barnsbury and Islington. When I got close to the canal, passing between Dalston and Hoxton, I saw a pack of dogs on a tiny patch of waste ground. With their ears pricked up they watched me go past and I was glad I was not on foot. I couldn't see anyone about, which seemed odd for a Sunday afternoon. I drove on.

Jaz's flat was tucked away somewhere between Hackney and Bethnal Green, on the second floor of a rundown building backing onto the canal. Different smells rose from the water in different seasons and at different times of the day, but not one of them was sweet.

The flat was large for one but Jaz had explained that was because it was hard to let and I could believe it. So much water came running down the bathroom wall you could take a shower in it, and there were constant scratching sounds which Jaz attributed to vermin without being any more specific. The doors to most of the flats were covered with graffiti. The communal stairs stank of rotting vegetables and animals. Rats, I hoped, because I hated them less than dogs.

I managed to get around to see Jaz maybe once a month. His building depressed me slightly but Jaz only ever wanted to meet there nowadays rather than in the Swan or the Queen's Head in Islington. The stairs made me nervous, so I always ran up, my boots clumping on the stone steps and echoing throughout the building.

Jaz was a while answering the door. 'I was in the darkroom,' he said when he finally appeared. Jaz was a freelance photographer. When we had met as couriers working for the same firm, Jaz took pictures as a hobby. Now, seven or eight years later, it was his livelihood. He'd done occasional fashion shoots and cookery features for the Sunday magazines, but he preferred working in the open air. His most recent project seemed to be all about grim photographs of urban landscapes.

'Hang on while I finish up in the darkroom,' he said as he disappeared, leaving me to close the door. The flat was back to its normal grand, lonely self. The last time I'd been there was for the party, when fifty or sixty people had been crammed into the high-ceilinged rooms and all the lights had been replaced by candles.

'Can I help?' I shouted to Jaz.

'Can you fuck,' came the reply, from behind the closed door at the end of the hall.

I wandered into the kitchen and looked out of the window. Two black dogs picked their way across the bomb site of a council block car-park. I felt the hairs on the back of my neck stand up. The dogs loped towards three young boys playing with pieces of brick. One of the boys hefted a half-brick and I thought he was going to attack one of the dogs. But the animals trotted past and the boy's half-brick came down on a beaten disc of metal, an old road sign by the look of it.

'Nice area, isn't it?' Jaz had joined me at the window. 'Which way did you come today?'

'Downham Road and Lee Street. Haggerston Road and over the canal.' The names lifted accurately from my mental map.

'Not the same though, is it? By car, I mean.' Jaz went to the fridge and took out a couple of beers. 'Not like on the bike. Like the old days.'

'You're right. I miss it.' Not strictly true, but I'll come to that. I moved away from the window and took my Camels from my boot and lit up, offering one to Jaz, who declined and levered the caps off the beers before handing one to me. Then he lit a Consulate, leaning back against the sink, and I grinned. 'Don't know how you can smoke those things,' I said. 'Like smoking Polos. Don't know how you can smoke at all. Filthy habit.'

'Too fucking right.' It was Jaz's turn to laugh. I'd been trying to give up on and off for some time.

Jaz went back to the window and I took a drag

on my cigarette. 'Where did you park your car?' Jaz asked. It was a joke. It wasn't funny but it was a joke. I knew that the car was parked right beneath where Jaz was standing, that he could see it from the window, and that he knew the car almost as well as he knew its owner. A Mark One dirty grey Escort with two missing wheel trims and a boot lid that wouldn't shut. The joke was it had been nicked. But I daresay you'd already worked that out.

'Pretty funny, Jaz,' I said from my end of the kitchen. 'No one would nick that car. It's a state, I know. But it gets me where I want to go.'

'So where's that?'

I looked around for an ashtray and decided the question wasn't worth answering. 'The other room,' I said sardonically. Jaz followed me through and again made straight for the windows. For someone who didn't like to leave his flat he sure liked the view. I went to the other window and put a foot up on the low ledge, staring across the canal at the iron latticework cradling two large, empty gasholders.

I moved away from the window and sank into one of the deep sheet-covered armchairs that were the only items of furniture in the large, bare-boarded room. On the walls were a couple of Jaz's favourite black-and-whites in cheap clipframes. There was a good one of me sitting on my bike near King's Cross looking a bit the worse for wear. I gripped the chilled bottle in my right hand and enjoyed the sensation. It was another warm day.

'That girl at your party,' I said casually while still looking out over the canal, 'what was her name? Ann, I think…'

'I think you mean Annie. And I think you know very well what she's called. Fucking hell, Carl, you stand out too much to be subtle.' He dragged on his Consulate. 'Have you been out with her then?'

I looked at Jaz. He was drinking and watching the scum drift on the surface of the canal. Was I really that transparent or had Jaz been unusually sensitive? For some reason I didn't want to go into details about Annie with Jaz. Some irrational mistrust or shyness held me back. However, I said: 'We went out, had a good time. But she's gone back to Manchester. Why does she want to live up there anyway?'

'You tell me, Carl. She's your babe.'

'She's not though. She made that quite clear. Didn't want to get involved. Wasn't interested. And yet,' I went on, 'I can't help thinking she was but she was hiding it or something.'

'Obviously,' Jaz said.

I lit another cigarette in response to this and arched my back as I settled deeper into the chair.

'You haven't got her number, have you, in Manchester?'

Jaz bounded across the room and I heard the darkroom door open. He returned with an old blue address book which was falling apart. He leafed through it. 'Have you got a pen?' he asked. I shook my head. 'Fucking hell. Do I have to do everything for you?' He got a pen from the kitchen and wrote the number on a piece of scrap paper, which he then passed to me. I held it tightly as if it were a hard-won secret or a key to the next stage in a complicated board game. Folding it in half I slipped it in the back pocket of my jeans.

Jaz was by the window again, watching the canal and the gasholders. 'How's the shop?' he asked.

'The shop?' I ran a small second-hand record shop on the Caledonian Road. I'd taken a lease on a former sex shop – a filthy, rank, dilapidated property – with the cash I'd saved from the courier job and various others, and started off by selling some of my own rare picture discs and limited editions: coloured vinyls, Bowie's foreign singles, Roxy Music's *Viva* on Island instead of Polydor. That sort of stuff. They were worth a fortune, some of them – things I'd collected in my youth – but I sold them for whatever I could get just to get through the first weeks. 'It's going OK,' I said. 'I thought I'd branch out. Sell a few second-hand books as well.'

'That should make your fortune.'

'Keeps me off the streets.'

The shop was doing OK. Surviving. It was like my life at the time. Everything was just sort of going along. Nothing major, good or bad. I felt like an engine that was idling, just waiting for someone or something to kick me into gear.

'You liked her then?' Jaz said, switching subjects. He was still staring at the canal, occasionally swigging beer. I should tell you what he looks like before you picture him all wrong. Shorter than me and stockier, he wore his dark, wavy hair cut short. His eyes were deep-set beneath prominent brows which made him look quite intense. He had a big nose and a beefy jaw. Like me he wore a lot of black.

'Yeah, I liked her,' I said.

Jaz went back to contemplating the canal. I swallowed another mouthful of beer and reached into my left boot.

I MET JAZ on my first day at City Circle Messengers. Desperate for a job in the hot summer of '83 or '84, I'd looked up courier companies in the Yellow

Pages and gone knocking on doors until one of them offered to take me on. City Circle were based in the scraggy grey area between King's Cross and the Angel, just off Pentonville Road in a vulnerable terrace of bookmakers, video shops and dressmakers surrounded by council blocks and cleared housing.

I climbed a greasy flight of stairs to reach their office. It was thick with acrid smoke that spiralled slowly in thrall to a big fan hanging down from the ceiling. A thin, sandy-haired man at the wrong end of his fifties, wearing a vest and a ropey old pair of headphones, sat behind a desk shouting adenoidally into a dented microphone. 'Alpha One Eight. Alpha One Eight. Where are you, One Eight? Come in, One Eight. Do you read me? Over.' Leave the poor bastard alone, I thought. Did I really want to work for this man? As I said, I was desperate.

Almost as pungent as the controller's Capstan Full Strength was his sweat. His name, I would learn later, was Anderton, but I would give him a different name: the Thin Controller. He had long insectile eyebrows and wore old glasses with grubby lenses and a wire frame that had been driven over by a bus and reassembled by a team of blind people with a roll of insulating tape. 'One Eight. Where are you, One Eight?… What the fuck are you doing there? You're supposed to be at number fourteen.' Another thing I would learn later was that regular client companies had numbers which you had to memorise. Fourteen was some PR agency in Victoria. I don't remember exactly where now. One Eight, it seemed, wasn't in Victoria. 'Do get a move on, One Eight,' he moaned sarcastically.

So the guy had a business to run and it depended on messengers turning up at the right place at the right time, but did he have to be such a complete twat to make it work? I didn't know, but I wished him dead. Stomach ulcer, throat cancer, whatever.

Also in the room were an obese, tough-looking woman in blue crimplene trousers and an orange T-shirt with strange stains down the front, and a huge black dog which skulked under the Thin Controller's desk. This disturbed me most of all. Then I noticed another messenger slumped in a plastic chair, playing with his two-way radio. His appearance and position in the chair made me think of an ape, but he was looking at me. It was a sympathetic look, almost a smile, and I was grateful for it. He might almost have been about to say, *Forget it, mate, don't work for this guy. He'll fuck you sideways.*

But I liked the look of his radio.

'Alpha Two Four. Two Four, Two Four, Two Four.'

The Thin Controller made some kind of signal in my direction, which the Fat Woman interpreted in her own way. 'You looking for work?' she asked me. I nodded, keeping a nervous eye on the black dog which had lifted its head and was slavering lazily. The Fat Woman got up, flesh shivering under the stress of walking. I hoped I would be able to stay out on the road and not have to call in at the office too often. The messenger sitting at the far end of the room drained a can of 7UP and tossed it into a wastebasket. The Thin Controller glared at him. The Fat Woman produced a form from under a mug stained with so much tannin it was black inside. I filled out my name, address and other details and signed some kind of disclaimer without bothering to read it. 'Where do I get my radio?' I asked.

The Thin Controller looked up. 'Listen to 'im. Wants his fucking radio. It's not a fucking holiday camp, you know.'

The Fat Woman steered me out of the office. Out of the corner of my eye I saw the other messenger watching me with amusement. In a tiny, nicotine-stained office down the landing, which smelt of worn-out house slippers and old files, the Fat Woman gave me a pad of dockets and a fluorescent bag. 'You have to wait two weeks till you get a radio,' she said. 'You have to phone in for jobs.'

This seemed a bit crap to me but I just nodded. It was a job. The Fat Woman then turned her attention to an in-tray overflowing with invoices and seemed to forget about me. I didn't know what to do. 'When do I start then?' I asked.

'What? Oh now. Today, I suppose.'

'Well, what's my first job?'

She looked up again and tutted. If they'd wanted a clairvoyant, they should have advertised. I mean, I didn't know where to go or what to do. She pushed past me – I held my breath – and I heard her mumbling to the Thin Controller in the other room. I picked out his nasal tones responding: 'Tell him to go to the West End and ring in.' I looked out through a jagged hole in the back window – the glass was too dirty to see through – and saw what looked like a tangle of rusty old bicycles in the weeds and rubble of the back yard.

The Fat Woman reappeared and I said, 'I heard.'

'What're you waiting for then?'

When I went out onto the street, the ape-like messenger was sitting on his bike at the side of the road. 'I'm Jaz,' he said. I said hello. In those days I didn't wear the boots and the white leather jacket. I dressed more quietly in torn jeans and fake Converse All Stars. Jaz had all the proper gear: black Lycra cycle shorts and a black sweat shirt. We wheeled our bikes down Pentonville Road together and he talked to me about City Circle and the creatures that ran it. 'Apparently they sleep together, those two,' he said, nodding back in the direction of the office. 'Horrible idea, isn't it? I think *she* joins in sometimes as well. His missus.' He was cracking jokes like this as soon as I met him. They weren't especially funny, but that was all right. He was a friendly face when I needed one.

I'd always wanted a brother, someone I could just hang out with. Just go somewhere and sit around with and for there to be no pressure. Someone who would help me out if I needed it. Wouldn't let me down.

Jaz wasn't necessarily that person. But the position was vacant.

Jaz showed me a few tricks. He told me never to phone in before I had to. The Thin Controller was not all that clued up and had no idea how long it took to cycle from, say, St Paul's to Kensington. So you could make the delivery in twenty minutes then have time for a coffee or a beer before calling in. The point was he *always* shouted at you for taking too long, even when you broke your neck to get somewhere quickly and rang in immediately. So there was no point stretching yourself for him. The incentive for zipping around from one place to another was that you could take a break on company time. The drawback was you got paid per job, so the more rests you took the less money you made, but money wasn't everything and taking advantage of the Thin Controller's stupidity was worth it in itself.

Jaz took me to Hanover Square and Soho Square, gathering points for couriers. You could meet people. There was a good atmosphere and a sense of solidarity. Most couriers had some horror story to tell, having narrowly escaped death-by-car-door-opener or themselves avoided killing passengers who stepped off buses in the middle of the road without looking.

I didn't enjoy the job as such and I hated having to speak to the Thin Controller on the phone but there was an aspect of the work that appealed to me. I had always loved maps, both for practical use and just for the pleasure of losing myself in them. If I wasn't reading a experimental French novel, then I'd have my nose in a map book. There really isn't that much difference. A map tells countless stories and, however crap it may sound, the novel – even one by Alain Robbe-Grillet or Michel Butor – can be a sort of large scale map of the human experience. Or maybe I just like the way things fit together. And the way they sometimes don't quite fit. What I did enjoy about the job were the times when I found myself between districts, leaving Maida Vale but not quite arriving in Kilburn. I could never decide if there was a gap between neighbouring areas or if they overlapped. I learned pretty quickly that they certainly didn't fit exactly. Borough boundaries might be precise – often running down the middle of a street – but real boundaries, those perceived by the people who live there, are not so fixed.

I pissed the Thin Controller off on only my second day. I'd just delivered a package in Southampton Row – and had a fifteen-minute rest in Russell Square – and I went looking for a phone box so I could call in. This was the summer of '83, remember, or '84, when the bookmakers were offering fifty-to-one odds against finding a public phone that worked, so I had to go quite a way. I called him eventually from an old red phone box somewhere east of Queen Square and he asked, 'Where are you, Two Three?' My call sign. Alpha Two Three. Jaz had told me the Thin Controller even had a number for the Fat Woman. And one for the dog.

I said, 'Somewhere between Bloomsbury and Clerkenwell.'

He gave a fruity cough, then said, 'This isn't a fucking guessing game, Two Three. Where are you?'

But I genuinely didn't know where I was. I knew London well. I wasn't lost. That's not what I mean. I mean I didn't know whether I was in Bloomsbury or Clerkenwell. I was too far east still to be in Bloomsbury proper and, surely, this far west I could hardly be in Clerkenwell.

'I don't know exactly, TC.'

'TC?'

'Er, The Controller.'

'Two Three, what's the fucking street called?'

I leaned backwards out of the phone box but couldn't see a street name. 'Can't see it, control. But I'm really quite close to Russell Square. Not far from Gray's Inn Road, not far from the office actually.'

Something really nasty crept into his voice now. 'Just find out exactly where you are, Two Three, and ring back. I can't waste time like this. You must think I'm made of money.'

'You're a cunt,' I said. After I'd hung up. What was he on about – made of money? I was paying for the fucking call.

The nice thing about all this was that I still didn't know where I was, Bloomsbury or Clerkenwell. Or some weird shadowland between the two, I might well have joked.

I used to wonder about places and how they came to be or ceased to be. There are names that hardly have places to belong to any more. Like Finsbury and Hornsey. There's a Hornsey High Street, a borough of Hornsey, a Hornsey Road and Hornsey Lane, but where the hell is Hornsey? You get there and all you find is a row of shops. There's no centre, no focus, no place.

Look down from the bridges you cross, however, and watch the railway lines that are carried over the road you're walking along. These are the transport routes in and out of places. But that's obvious. Railway lines, canals, wasteland stretching into the distance. What I'm saying is, so much of what surrounds us is hidden from view. We have to look for it. And if you look hard enough you'll find it. It's there. Everything's there somewhere and anything's possible. Honestly. I know.

JAZ WAS STILL staring at the canal. I lit a cigarette and the flare of the match caught his attention. He went into the kitchen and shouted, 'Another beer?' as he opened the fridge door.

'One more, then I must go,' I said.

He returned with two beers and sat opposite me in one of the other big chairs. For a moment it seemed as if there was nothing to say.

I hadn't told Jaz about the incident with the phone in the house and the caller asking for me. In fact, whereas at the time it seemed as if the call were intended for me, by now I was thinking maybe I'd just stumbled across an odd coincidence. And perhaps the reason why I didn't mention it to Jaz was because of his habit of saying the wrong thing. He might have made some flippant remark which would have irritated me. He often seemed uncomfortable with anything that wasn't clear-cut and black and white like his photographs. For the time being I put the matter out of my mind.

I left Jaz's flat soon after the second beer. On my way downstairs I paused at a south-facing window. The sun's rays struck the gasholders' cradles almost horizontally and made them glow a deep ruddy gold. I knew that particular angle of light would last no longer than a minute or two. For some reason it seemed like a good omen to have caught it. I thought about standing there and enjoying the view until the sun went down, but decided the omen would lose its potency if I watched the gasholders slip into shadow. I slipped out of the building and crossed to my car, Annie Risk's phone number in my back pocket.

Chapter Three

THAT EVENING WHEN I got back to the flat I was too tired to do anything except collapse in front of the television. I channel-hopped – through an old black and white movie with lots of stark lighting and cigarette smoke, a 70s TV movie featuring actors I recognised but couldn't put names to, and a political discussion which went around and around and got nowhere – until I settled down to ice-skating coming from somewhere in Europe. In fact, it doesn't matter where it's actually coming from because it always seems like Europe, either high in the alps or up in Scandinavia or Russia or somewhere else cold and icy. It's all quite simple really.

The thing about ice-skating is not only do skaters desire to break their own records as well as matching themselves against the competition, but also they long to surpass what is accepted as possible in their field. Occasionally they strain at the barriers of what is humanly possible. When they jump, they're hoping for a triple salchow, or axel or lutz. Quadruples are rare. I once saw a quadruple toe loop, by a French woman in the Winter Olympics. I remember her face as she landed: it was ecstatic, but there was a look in her eye of something close to madness.

Watching ice-skating always reminded me of my favourite track by my favourite band, 'Watching You Dance' by the Passage, a group that emerged from Manchester's soot and shadows just before I left for London in the early 80s: Dick Witts' whispered vocal about an unnamed dancer shooting through the air, escaping the earth.

I dragged myself to the fridge to get a cold Sapporo, then collapsed in front of the skating. When a skater goes into a triple lutz she throws everything into it. The judges might not require her to jump a quadruple, but that's what she's straining for. She wants to stay up there a little bit longer; like a ballet dancer, she wants to fly, escape the earth. Only it's not possible. It's not *supposed to be* possible. But it doesn't stop her wanting it. And it doesn't stop me wanting it for her. I watch ice-skating and I'm emotionally drained; my body aches in sympathy.

They jumped and span. They landed; one or two stumbled. One guy skated into the barrier and fell over, hurting his knee, but carried on to do a triple toe loop and a double axel. The crowd loved him. He was crying as he bowed. Me too. Christ, I was bawling my eyes out. I suddenly realised I was thinking about Annie Risk and the evening we'd had together; the kiss. Fuck it. I'd got her number, why not use it? I reached behind the sofa for the phone. It was on the floor, strangled by its own curly flex. I fished the scrap of paper out of my jeans and punched in the digits. As I waited for the connection I had second, third and fourth thoughts. It was late. I was being too keen. Spur-of-the-moment decisions invariably land me in the shit. I returned the handset to the cradle. It seemed more sensible just to go to bed.

A that moment the phone rang, startling me. I was still holding it in my lap so I grabbed the receiver. 'Hello? Hello?'

There was no answer.

'Annie,' I tried, thinking that somehow she had known it was me ringing a moment before. No reply. I said hello a couple more times only to hear those strange metallic grating and echoing sounds you hear on these occasions. No one there. I replaced the receiver and sat staring at the phone for a while before deciding to go to bed.

The alarm woke me at eight in the morning. Taking a cigarette from the pack next to the bed I lit up and lay back against the pillows. Breakfast. I thought about the day ahead as I looked around the bedroom. The walls held posters of Siouxsie, John Lee Hooker and Lenin, and the covers of the first two Passage LPs, *Pindrop* and *For All and None*. There was also a faded picture of the 1971 Manchester City squad and a clipframed photograph of me and Jaz freewheeling down Ludgate Hill. He'd set the camera up on a tripod and we'd got it just right first time.

Cigarette finished, I visited the bathroom, then pulled on my tight black jeans and a red sweatshirt and lit another cigarette while I made coffee. I had a loaf of bread somewhere and boxes of cereal. I don't know why because I never had more than black coffee and cigarettes for breakfast. I took my coffee into the living room and sat back on the huge low-slung sofa. There was a big glass ashtray overflowing on the coffee table between piles of videos and record sleeves and books. All around the room, and out into the hallway, the walls were shelved to take my collection of records and CDs. I didn't know how many there were. Thousands. Books, there weren't so many. My tastes were quite narrow. Cult fiction, anything published by John Calder or Peter Owen or Marion Boyars; compilations of *Daily Telegraph* crossword puzzles; road atlases, map books, A–Zs.

I parked the car a couple of streets away from the shop. There was no good reason why I did that. I'd done it once and it became a habit. There had been space in front of the shop but I'd chosen not to use it. Maybe I just wanted a short walk before the day began.

I paused briefly to light up. There was that sense of anticipation you get at the beginning of a fine summer's day; a slight breeze turned drink cartons and leaflets for carpet warehouses over in my path. I took a drag on my cigarette and it must have been too deep because my head started to swim. I stopped walking to let it clear. It did, but for a moment my senses seemed strangely heightened. Everything around me had become more vivid. A bright post box, a tree in bloom, which I passed every morning but noticed now for the first time, was an explosion of colour, a gleaming black Mini that drove past with a single occupant whose black hair shone like Siouxsie Sioux's or Andy Wilson's from the Passage – or my mother's.

The breeze whistled past my ears and carried a slight tang that I failed to identify. I could hear individual scraps of paper grate against the pavement.

I thought to myself that I should consider switching to Camel Lights or those yellow Silk Cut that had so little tar in them they arguably didn't exist.

The sensation lasted only a couple of seconds and as it passed and I rubbed my eyes and shook my head I saw the map at my feet. It appeared to be a page photocopied from an A–Z. In black and white, printed only on one side, frayed at the edges and scored with deep folds, it looked as if it had been blowing about for a while. I picked it up and had a proper look. Mildly interesting, I thought, assuming it to represent part of North London, and I slipped it into the back pocket of my jeans with Annie Risk's phone number.

When I reached the shop there were two or three kids hanging around waiting for it to open. I greeted them and they grunted back. My customers kept me in Camels and takeaways from the Hong Kong Garden, the Chinese place two floors beneath my flat. It wasn't really called that. The real name didn't roll off the tongue as easily and wasn't a Siouxsie and the Banshees song title.

One of the kids who'd been waiting wanted Toy Planet's first LP on Spoon Records which was so rare even I didn't have a copy. Not in the shop anyway. I had a copy at home but that was mine, bought from a little place in Brighton some years before. He wasn't having that. I occasionally took home records I bought from punters in the shop, but only rarely did I sell anything from my own collection.

I recommended Can. He looked doubtful. 'It's the same guy,' I said and he brightened up, leaving with a copy of *Tago Mago* for not much more than I'd paid for it.

There was a quiet period during which I looked over the latest addition to the shop – the single shelf of second-hand books I'd mentioned to Jaz. I'd gone for a limited range of titles that both reflected my taste and projected a particular image. So there were some Penguin Modern Classics, a few Picadors – Knut Hamsun, William Burroughs, *The Existential Imagination*, *The Naked I* – and anything I could

find by Anna Kavan, Alan Burns, Boris Vian and
Alain Robbe-Grillet. It probably didn't fit with
the whole cowboy boots and leather jacket look I
affected, but I was a sucker for the *nouveau roman*.
The only trouble was my extremely limited French,
which was where John Calder's translated editions
came in.

The LP that was playing came to an end and I
replaced it with the second Passage album, *For All
and None*. I dropped the needle down at the start of
track two, 'Lon Don', the Manchester band's caustic
demolition of the capital.

I remembered the map in my back pocket and was
about to get it out when a man in a brown suede
bomber jacket came in with a box of old singles
he wanted to sell. While I was dealing with him
the shop slowly started to fill up. I bought all the
singles – evidently stuff he'd bought in the 70s, as an
enthusiast, and had grown out of – and I bought them
even though many were already in stock, because I
don't like to send people away disappointed. When
the record came to an end I turned it over. I lost count
of how many times I turned it over during the rest of
the day and I didn't think about the map again until
I locked the door and flipped the open/closed sign. I
was reaching into my back pocket for Annie's number
because I'd thought I would give her a call and I
pulled out the map. Unfolding it for the first time
since that morning, I sniffed it. There was a strange,
pungent odour detectable beneath the familiar smell
of my jeans. Or I thought there was. An industrial
smell, almost. Railways or diesel oil. Engines. But I
was losing myself. The main thing was the map.

I looked at it for a minute or two but couldn't
work out where it represented. So I switched off

the main light and went into the back office where I made coffee, pulled the anglepoise lamp down over the desk and lit a cigarette.

I studied that map. I gave it twenty minutes' solid concentration. I don't give up easily once I feel I'm on to something. I'd always enjoyed crossword puzzles, word games, Scrabble. It's the challenge of figuring out something to which you *know* there is an answer. It's just a question of working it out.

I knew North London well enough to be certain it was not north of the river and my knowledge of South, East and West London was good enough to be fairly sure it was, in fact, nowhere in the capital. And yet it looked like someone had needed to go somewhere and they had taken the A–Z and photocopied a page to take with them because they didn't want to carry the whole thing. Then they'd dropped their page in the street. A London street, which would suggest they were going somewhere in London. But it wasn't London. By the end of twenty minutes I was confident enough to put money on it being out of town. I'd been looking for clues in the street names to what provincial city it might be part of, but there was nothing, no mention of the Tyne or the Potteries, no name check for the Malverns, the Chilterns or the Peaks. There weren't any obvious Irish, Scots, Welsh or Cornish names. They were all bland, English street names. I'd walked down several of them in different cities but not on the same page.

I would have to look at my A–Zs when I got home.

At this stage the map was just a diversion, a puzzle that I expected would keep me occupied for a day or two until I found out whereabouts in the country the streets on it were located. It looked like an area quite close to a city centre. Some of the roads were densely packed. There were long straight drives and grids of narrow streets. There was a park, a canal and railway lines and I would have said from the movement towards the top of the page that the city centre lay just to the north. An inch south of where it started getting busy there was an estate where the streets curved around and around like that game of solitaire where you have to get the ball to the middle of the maze. There was even a little circle at the centre.

I stubbed out my second cigarette, put the map back in my pocket and switched off the light. I sat for a moment looking through the doorway into the darkened shop. Passing cars splashed light over the racks of dog-eared LP sleeves, flashing in the CD cases in the wall-mounted display units. I liked the silence after the continuous noise of the day. I have always liked busy places best when they are empty. It's partly because I'm there and all the other people are not, and partly it's that although they've gone they're still very much in mind because of the traces they leave: echoes, memories, smells, a door left open, a dropped glove or, in the case of my shop, a misfiled LP sleeve or a list written in felt tip that says, 'Only Ones, Dead or Alive, P. Furs, The Servant(?)'.

I hesitated at the door. It had started to rain. Rear lights melted into red pools as cars braked for the stop sign. I hoped the original owner of the map fragment wasn't wandering around getting wet and hopelessly lost. Then, as I was turning the key in the lock to let myself out, the phone began to ring. I thought about leaving it because the shop was closed, but it was possible it was someone who'd tried me at home and wanted to get hold of me.

I left the door unlocked and darted back into the little office.

'Hello,' I said, and as soon as I'd said it I knew there was no one there. I heard that same metallic sound I'd heard on the phone at home the night before. Then a whole train of olfactory hallucinations kicked in. I imagined I could smell axle grease and diesel oil and the peculiar tang of rusty cast iron.

My imagination, I told myself as I got up to go. As I was leaving the office, my eye alighted on an old tool box I'd stashed under the desk a few weeks earlier after I'd been doing some emergency repair-work on the car. There was an oily rag sticking out of the top section. I smiled to myself. Imagination overload. I nipped up the back stairs to use the toilet.

Walking to my car I realised I was looking twice at everything I saw, watching taxis and buses and pedestrians. As if I were looking for something without knowing what.

The rain had stopped but my car was covered with droplets. From a distance of thirty yards, because of the streetlamp directly above it, it looked as if it were encrusted with jewels. Once I was behind the wheel I took the pack of Camels from my boot and hit the lighter in the dash. The car started on the third attempt and the lighter clicked out. I raised it to my cigarette, averting my eyes from the glowing spiral filament.

I drove home slowly, avoiding puddles wherever possible because the engine on the Escort did not react well to direct contact with water. The Hong Kong Garden looked inviting – as it did every night of the week – so I went in and ordered hot and sour soup and fried chicken with pineapple and waited while it was prepared.

I was halfway through my dinner when I remembered the map. I didn't know why I kept forgetting it. Five minutes later I had the map open on the coffee table, the London A–Z, my food and a can of Sapporo. Things were looking up. I went right through the A–Z, checking every page. I picked out a couple of the street names from the map and tried them out on the A–Z index. They were in there, but not on the same page.

Finally I was satisfied that what I had already believed was indeed the case. The streets on the map were nowhere to be found in London.

I also had A–Zs for Birmingham, Manchester and Newcastle. Before looking for them – I wasn't entirely sure where they were – I stuck on a CD. Something by Vangelis seemed right, just to play in the background while I got on with my search. I chose *The City*, because it seemed kind of appropriate, and turned the volume low. The downstairs tenant was out – I was on the second floor at the top of the building, there was one tenant on the first floor and the Hong Kong Garden occupied the ground floor. I was glad he was out. When he was in, my life was like a film with a heavy metal soundtrack.

I found the other A–Zs on a bookshelf in the bathroom and spent half an hour or so looking through them before concluding that the streets on the map were not to be found in Birmingham, Manchester or Newcastle.

Obsessive behaviour? I guess so, but to me it didn't seem all that different from trying to complete a crossword puzzle. It occupied my mind and stopped me thinking about Annie Risk. I took out a road atlas and pored over that for a while, studying the city centre street maps in the back and glancing through the place names in the index.

The following evening, after I'd locked up the shop around 6pm, I drove into town, parked up by Russell Square and walked over to Charing Cross Road. I had the map in my pocket and an hour or so in hand before the bookshops closed. In a succession of basements, enveloped by the smell of new books, I checked the indexes of every A–Z and every street plan for all the major towns and cities in the UK. I checked Cork and Dublin. The map didn't figure anywhere. I'd ruled out Australia and America and former colonies.

It was 9.30pm when I arrived home, which I thought sounded like a pretty good time to phone Annie Risk. It was likely she would tell me to fuck off but I couldn't just let it go.

I rang the number and she answered. The conversation went something like this.

'Aw, go on.'

'No.'

She wasn't interested in a relationship. She'd recently broken up with someone and the experience had left her wary of men in general. She wasn't ready to try again. I said there'd be no pressure, no commitments on either side, we'd see each other when we both wanted to etc. 'Doesn't sound like much of a relationship,' she said. Oh, and she said no. She kept on saying no.

The thing was I could see her point of view. He sounded like a dick, the one she'd broken up with. Just like me. He'd promised her all sorts of things and let her down.

'Men,' I said.

'Exactly,' she responded. 'Which doesn't help your case very much, does it?' She was not wrong. I let her go on talking. It might sound crap but I liked the sound of her voice. She lived in Manchester but had been brought up in Nottingham and her accent came from there. If she was in a film she'd keep saying 'duck'. She didn't call me 'duck' but I'd been out with a Nottingham girl before so I recognised the intonation. That relationship hadn't lasted very long. None of my relationships had. It's more to do not just with meeting the right person, but with meeting the right person at the right time. And not being fucked up with certain 'issues' helps, too. Apparently.

'I think we'd be good together,' I told her. 'You with your cynicism and me just kind of rolling along. I'm not going to try and control you.' That's what you say at times like this, isn't it? And you mean it too.

'But I want to be controlled,' she said. She was difficult to get a handle on, Annie Risk.

'Do you play Scrabble?' I asked, changing the subject with the deftness of a politician. 'We could play Scrabble.'

'Interesting idea,' she said with heavy sarcasm. 'Beats going out and having a good time. Anyway, you'd win.'

'No I wouldn't. I'm rubbish at Scrabble. I'm no good at most things. I just enjoy doing them.'

'That's nice,' she said. She was giving me a bit of a hard time and I supposed that was fair enough because I was putting her under some pressure. We talked for another five minutes.

'Can I ring you again?' I asked her.

'Yes,' she said. 'I like talking to you.'

So, I hadn't got a result but I'd got something – a goalless draw maybe – which was better than nothing and I was happy with that for the time being. A score draw, perhaps. Away.

Excited, I prowled around the flat. I trailed my fingers along the spines of hundreds of LPs and slid out one or two at random. About a third of my collection had been bought second-hand, either through the shop or before all that started. I could spend hours just looking through the shelves, not necessarily playing any records, just looking at the sleeves and occasionally slipping the record out to smell the vinyl and read the inscription, if any, etched into the runout groove by the cutting engineer at his lathe.

I took down a 12 inch single – *IV Songs* by In Camera – and had a look at the inscription scratched into the runout groove: 'Thanks Ilona'. Inscribed on the original acetate by the cutting engineer, these messages fascinated me; they were clues to a world of secrets and hidden relationships that existed behind or beyond the record. I put the In Camera single back.

It was late and I was tired. I went to get another beer from the fridge and played a couple of old Banshees tracks. I took a cigarette from the pack on the coffee table and looked around for my lighter. It wasn't on the table, nor in my jacket pockets, nor my left boot. I rummaged in the kitchen drawer but I appeared to be out of matches. My last resort – and I took it reluctantly – was to use the electric ring on the cooker. I'd never liked old-fashioned electric rings.

I was four or five. My mother was cooking in the kitchen and I was sitting on the orange plastic seat watching her. We were company for each other while my father was out doing shift work. My mother was mixing ingredients in a dish on the work surface and her beautiful black hair fell from behind her ear, forming a temporary curtain between us. She would no longer have been able to see me out of the corner of her eye. But I was keeping quiet and she knew I was all right. She never really had to worry about me. Until that evening. Maybe I was restless because I no longer had even half her attention. Whatever. I placed my hand on top of the edge of the cooker to pull myself up out of the chair. Then without looking I placed my hand flat on the electric ring, the idea being to take my body weight and swing from the chair onto the surface where my mother was working.

But the ring was on. My mother had put it on in readiness for the dish she was preparing. It was bright orange. I seemed to hang in mid-air for eternity before I screamed. My mother jumped and whirled around. I'm not sure I can describe the pain. It shot up my arm and my head felt as if it were in a vice. Next thing I knew I was on the floor and my mother was screaming but nobody else came. She held my little hand delicately and tried to uncurl my fingers. They were shut tight as if I had something secret in my hand I didn't want to show anyone. By now my head was swimming. She managed to open my hand and I looked. A dark brown spiral covered my palm. For the first time in my life, I smelt burnt flesh.

It took months for the scar to fade.

So, when I moved into the flat and discovered it came with an electric cooker, I promised myself I would replace it, but I never did.

When the ring had heated up sufficiently and was already an orange blur – I tried not to look at it directly – I swept my long hair away from my face and bent over the ring with the cigarette in my mouth. In the coils of my mind I heard the Passage sing about gas and electricity in 'Shave Your Head', the smell, the burning. Instead of switching the cooker off like an intelligent person would have done I watched the ring get hotter and hotter and brighter and brighter. It smelt dark and sharp, becoming more intense the hotter it got. It was like vertigo: you're scared of heights precisely because you're attracted to them. It took an effort of will to switch the ring off and leave the kitchen.

I returned to the main room and had a swig of beer. The very best way to round off the evening, I decided, given that I wasn't going to get any further with the map when I was this tired, was watching Siouxsie. I'd recorded the 'Kiss Them For Me' video off the TV. I stretched out on the sofa and watched her dance. When you've had enough beers and you're already quite tired, it's not difficult to convince yourself she's in the room and dancing and singing just for you. It helps if you put the lights out and if you've got a decent-sized TV. There's nothing worse than a small TV.

I kept watching until I was too tired to rewind it back to the beginning each time. The way she moved in that video made me feel less lonely. I went to bed tired but unable to sleep. I reached for my book – Robbe-Grillet's *Un Régicide* – and found my place and tried very, very hard to pick up the story. Although *Un Régicide* was Robbe-Grillet's first novel, written in 1949, it was not published until 1978, and so was something like his ninth or

tenth to appear depending on whether you regard
La Belle Captive as a novel, and then only in French.
There still had been no English translation, so I was
struggling through it with my A-level French, largely
forgotten.

The action kept switching between an unnamed
modern city and a mist-cloaked island. I couldn't
quite work out if Boris, who was a factory worker
in the city, was meant to be the same person as the
unnamed narrator of the island sections. It was
probably not the best thing to read at the end of a
long day. I managed half a page before the narrator's
stumbling around lost in the mist began to reflect my
own vain attempts to focus my attention.

Chapter Four

AND THIS IS what happened *after*.

I thought about the map constantly while serving customers and sorting through boxes of scratchy singles and unwanted albums. It wasn't that I was bored of my customers' frequent complaints and demands for a few extra quid, but that the business of running the shop was no longer sufficient to distract me from thinking about Annie Risk.

I'd tried again, a couple more times, ringing her up in the evening after work when I hoped she'd be relaxed and receptive to my ideas. We got on fine, because I let her go ahead and take the piss, but that was as far as it was going to go, she said.

With each phone call I fell deeper and deeper into whatever it was I was feeling for her. Perhaps the map represented an escape route from this frustration. Something else to think about.

An original '76 punk with bad teeth and nailed boots clumped into the shop and said he wanted £25 for the Skids' 'Into the Valley' on white vinyl and £30 for the *Wide Open* EP, twelve inch on red. I suggested he'd do better to advertise in the music papers. I'd already got two copies of one and three of the other in the shop and no one seemed to want to buy them.

'What about Roxy Music *Viva!* on Island? Forty quid.'

'I've got three in stock.'

'Not on Island,' the punk argued. 'It's rare.'

'It's rare but I've got three of them.'

I was lying. Instinctively I'd decided not to buy anything at all off the punk. I didn't like the look of him. I had nothing against punks. I liked them if they were clean and looked as if they could communicate without the aid of violence, but this guy looked like he hadn't changed his bondage trousers or washed his hair since the Sex Pistols told Bill Grundy to fuck off.

He had a quick sulky flick through the new wave section before slinking out of the shop.

I took the map out and studied the layout of the streets. Bending down slightly behind the till I shut my eyes and ran my fingers over the paper to see if that would yield anything. But all I felt were the slight ridges of toner from the photocopier. Out of the corner of my eye I noticed two young girls playing peek-a-boo with me from behind the soundtracks section. Did they know anything about the map? Was it a deliberate plant? Or was I getting paranoid? Just possibly.

I stepped forward to the till to serve a boy buying a clutch of house singles and when I looked up again the girls had gone. When I gave it some thought, I realised a great many people passed through the shop, trailing their lives and their secrets, and some of what they carried tended to get left behind. When I shut the shop every night the atmosphere was a little bit richer. The records contained so many memories, good and bad, different jokes for different folks. Had I bought the Skids singles off the punk, I would have taken part of him into my shop to stay after the doors were locked. Perhaps that was why I'd said no.

Maybe the answer to the map was somewhere in the shop, left in some customer's wake. If I searched through the racks I would perhaps discover that the LP sleeves had been refiled in some arcane pattern. I looked carefully at the records I had bought during the morning in case their titles revealed anything. But there was nothing. Obviously. I played a random selection of singles and listened with one ear to the lyrics.

The book shelf had started to receive a bit of attention. I'd sold a copy of Anna Kavan's *Ice* – the Picador edition with the ghostly painted nude on the front cover – to a girl with sharp little teeth and enormous blue eyes. I ran my fingers along the spines and took out a copy of Robbe-Grillet's *In the Labyrinth* that had been put back under G instead of R. I flicked through the pages, lifting it to my nose. Beneath the smells of tobacco and tea I could pick up something else, something industrial. I got a flash of one of Jaz's pictures.

'Excuse me.'

'What? Sorry. Yes?'

'How much is this?'

I looked at a guy in front of me in little round glasses holding a copy of the Banshees' 'Mittageisen' single in a picture sleeve.

'Give us a quid,' I said.

Customers came and went steadily until it started to rain late in the afternoon and then, if anything, it got even busier.

I knew I could make something up out of all the material at my fingertips, but I would know I'd invented it. If a genuine message were to emerge I'd know it because I'd feel it. So I thought.

By the end of the day I felt saturated with images and voices and longed for abstraction and silence. The roads were empty. The Escort's tyres hissed on wet tarmac and I cruised with the radio off. It had got dark early because of the rainclouds. The red lights in the distance became a cascade of reflections in the puddles as I knocked the gear lever into neutral and coasted down to meet them. I used to do this a lot, imagining it saved petrol. On one occasion I'd switched off the engine as well and rolled silently through the night. I got a fright when I turned the wheel and the steering lock engaged. I just managed to turn the key again before running into a lamppost. That was the last time I tried that trick.

I rolled into position behind a girl in a Mini who, like me, was waiting for the lights to change. She had shoulder-length black hair like Siouxsie Sioux – and indeed like Annie Risk – and was bobbing up and down on her seat and moving from side to side, tapping her fingers on the steering wheel and banging the dash.

I suddenly wanted to know what she was listening to, in case it was a clue. The longer the lights stayed on red and she continued to bounce up and down the more strongly I felt it. My stomach twisted around and around. If only I could hear what she was listening to, then I'd share her secret and perhaps I'd know the way to drive to the streets on the map.

I wound my window down but her window was up and I couldn't hear anything. The little car moved in sympathy with her, as if it were her cocoon. I couldn't pull alongside because there was only one lane.

The lights changed and she was off. I jerked into first and followed, reaching across to switch on the radio to see if she was listening to a station I could tune into. The gap between us lengthened as I slewed across the dial, stopping to catch fragments of music. But there was nothing that spoke to me as clearly as the girl's movements. It must have been a tape. She was a long way ahead now. I jumped a red light to keep her in sight but she turned into a side street and although I followed, she vanished into a warren of crescents I barely knew.

When I got in I tried Annie's number but she was either not in or not answering. I got some food from downstairs, had a couple of beers and several cigarettes. It was an evening like any other. I sat on the floor idly looking through my white-labels.

At the shop I used to buy a lot of white label promos in blank sleeves from collectors and if there were any I wanted to keep I just took them home. It was all the same money, whether it was at the shop or at home. Lots of them had the artist's name scrawled across the white label in felt tip, but some were blank and these were the ones I liked best because if there were no distinguishing marks I could forget who the record was by and playing it was always a surprise.

I pulled a couple out of their sleeves and studied them for clues. Nothing to do with the map, this, just clues as to who the records were by. I put one on and still couldn't work it out. I sometimes bought stuff without knowing what it was. Maybe I should have got one of those signs for the shop: "You don't have to be mad to work here but it helps."

I fell asleep on the sofa and woke with a start when my cigarette had burned right down and stung my finger. I sucked at it as I drew my legs off the table and stood up. In the bathroom I ran my finger under the cold tap and examined it under the light over the mirror. There was a tiny patch where the whorls of my fingerprint had been smoothed over. Fascinated, I stared at the pattern of parallel lines. On the third finger of my right hand the lines seemed to fan out in a spiral from a central point, like the way hair grows from the crown. But, even though I was on a second wind, I realised that when you've got down to examining your own fingerprints it's time to say goodnight.

I was smoking and reading *Un Régicide* in bed when the front door rattled in its frame. With a clear view of the door from my bed, I looked up and put my book down beside me. When the door opened I wasn't altogether surprised to see the girl from the car. Her black hair framed a face that was Siouxsie's, except that it wasn't. Because it was Annie Risk's. But it wasn't hers either: the hair was too low over the forehead. She was like a composite of both of them. The only two women in my life, both very much on its fringes, synthesized into this one girl.

She walked in and turned past the bedroom doorway to enter the living room. I followed her. She went over to my stereo and slipped a single from inside her denim jacket onto the turntable. She stood back and I came forward to see what she'd brought. A white label disc was spinning at 45 rpm and the needle cut into it. I looked up but the girl had gone. I whirled around and ran to the door but it was shut and there was no sound in the stairwell. I bent over the record player again and saw that as the needle travelled around the groove towards the centre it left a fine spiral of raspberry-coloured liquid in its wake.

I woke up. My cigarette had burnt a hole in the duvet cover. I smothered it quickly with a pillow, but there was no need: the cigarette was cold. I felt sick and shivered. Brushing the curtain behind my head to one side I looked down into the street for a Mini, but there was only my Escort and one or two other familiar cars.

I checked the front door – undisturbed – and the stereo. There was no record on the turntable and no blood anywhere – naturally – but the power was on. I never left the power on. I flicked the switch and went to use the bathroom. I decided my subconscious had known I'd left the power on and so I'd dreamt about it.

I went back to bed but couldn't get back to sleep, so I got up and pulled on a pair of boxer shorts and went through to the living room. A cigarette and the Siouxsie video. It was a combination that never failed to engender pleasure, but if I'd wanted to become either completely relaxed or tired enough to go back to sleep I would have been disappointed. My body was exhausted but my brain was active. At dawn I was thinking of taking the car for a run down to the crescent where I'd lost the girl in her Mini when I finally fell asleep in front of the TV.

Driving to the shop a couple of hours later I felt like a jigsaw puzzle that had been put together wrongly. Someone had tried to force pieces into each other and they held, but only just. I had a craving for fresh orange juice but made do with a cigarette instead. I pushed in the dashboard lighter and waited for it to pop out. I withdrew it and brought it up to my mouth. While driving I looked down to align the end of the cigarette with the lighter and my eye was drawn to the burning orange element. I lost my grip on the steering wheel and went the wrong way around a set of bollards. Instantly nauseated, I righted the car and coasted to the kerb. I got out, threw the cigarette in the gutter and leaned against the bonnet for a few moments. The shop would have to open late for once.

I kept seeing the needle cutting into the record and drawing blood. I climbed into the car and got back on the road. Every Mini turned my head. I'd never noticed them before but now it seemed like the city streets were full of them. I couldn't remember what colour the Siouxsie/Annie girl had been driving. It had, after all, been dark.

I imagined, during the hours of daylight, it parked up in one of the streets on my map. Only by night did she venture into the light of the real world.

I struggled to concentrate on the business of running the shop. The jigsaw feeling had faded but I still wasn't on top form. I chainsmoked and played randomly selected singles back to back all morning. Customers brought me boxes of records and I bought them all with the briefest examinations and without haggling. The shop was infested with Siouxsie clones but they were all years out of date, painted dolls and scarecrows, their faces plastered with the Halloween make-up Siouxsie herself now did without. Over the years, as the masks had been slowly stripped away she had become more and more beautiful to the point where her beauty was now a provocation, like the music had always been.

I slipped *Superstition* into the CD player and pressed repeat.

In a stream of people offering me their old picture discs and limited edition gatefold sleeves a girl's hand pushed a white label single onto the counter. I gave a small cry and immediately looked up but the floor was crowded with customers. Out of the corner of my eye I saw the door close, but it could have been anybody. Nevertheless, I squeezed under the counter and pushed through the crowd to the door. I craned my neck and looked in all directions but she had disappeared. There was no sign of a Mini parked nearby. Heart pounding, I re-entered the shop.

Word must have got around that I was throwing money away today: it seemed as if the whole teenage population of the city had descended on the shop. 'Whose is this?' I asked, holding up the white label. No one claimed it. 'Is it yours?' I asked the next girl in the queue. She nodded. Someone behind her cackled like a hyena and I felt foolish, but for all I knew it could really have been hers and she'd been too shy to stick her hand up. The colour of the label could have prompted me to imagine someone who hadn't been there at all. I took the other stuff the girl clearly hadn't been expecting to sell, then lit a cigarette and put the white label underneath a stack of CDs to look at later.

It was with relief that I locked the door and flipped the open/closed sign. I didn't need this. I stood and watched the rain through the glass as I lit a cigarette and put the lighter away in my jacket pocket. Cars squealed softly as they braked for the red light. I smoked nervously, unhappy about acknowledging my fear of the unknown girl and the white label. In the brightness of the afternoon it had been easier to rationalise. I watched car headlamps dazzle and melt into wet reflections like silver waterfalls. Taking a deep drag that caused my head to spin I turned away from the window and went back to the counter. I felt like a bug in a killing jar. They could be watching me through the windows from across the street. They would want to see how I reacted when I listened to the white label.

I slipped it out of its blank sleeve, holding it by the edges and angling it so that the light fell across it. There was nothing written on the label, but on the runout groove I made out the inscription 'It's a gas'. It meant nothing to me. Just some cutting engineer's throwaway remark.

I placed the record on the turntable with care and positioned the needle before pressing release. It landed with that satisfying clunk I had heard a million times. It doesn't matter how new a vinyl record is, you always hear something apart from what you're meant to hear, even if it's only the hiss of dust. I wondered what I would actually hear, as the needle wound its way towards the music.

But none came. I checked the amp controls. Everything was on and the volume was turned up. I looked at the needle. It was a third of the way into the record and still there was no sound.

I turned the volume higher and listened more intently. There was the usual rumble of ticks and bumps you get at the beginning and end of records. When it finished I repositioned the needle and played it again. With the volume full up I fancied I could hear the needle itself scoring the groove a fraction deeper. I found myself becoming drawn to the sound. Without the distraction of music it was somehow purer, more elemental. I played the flip side and it was the same. The more I played it and the harder I listened, the more it sank into me. I noticed also that my forehead had begun to hurt where the skin stretched tightly across it. A sharp irritating pain like a paper cut.

Pain or no pain I was in thrall to the record. I loved its silence and slowly I began to make out the sounds that *were* there to be heard if you listened hard enough. I played it again and again until I felt I was in a waking dream.

Towards midnight I locked up and walked to the car, the white label in a padded envelope under my arm. I laid it carefully on the passenger seat and started the engine. I drove like an automaton, wide, dry eyes sweeping the road ahead in search of the girl's car. I felt I knew now what she'd been dancing to. I'd felt like dancing myself. In the shop. Listening to the record over and over again. It was as if the walls and ceiling had receded and I had felt myself at the centre of a huge spiral descending upon me from the sky.

Waiting at a red light, rain stippling the windscreen, I pressed in the cigarette lighter and reached into my boot. I stuck a cigarette between my lips. The lighter popped out and I withdrew it. I stared at the burning spiral for a few moments before inserting the third finger of my left hand into the barrel of the lighter and pressing the tip against the element. I didn't blink. Rain fell more heavily on the car, beating a tinny tattoo on the roof. The light went green but I didn't move. An acrid smell of charred flesh filled the car.

I only pulled my finger away when I felt my nail grating unpleasantly against the metal coil.

My finger was black, my face in the rearview mirror as blank as a piece of paper. The light was red again. I replaced the cigarette lighter and waited for the light to change. When it did I shifted into first gear, wincing as my finger brushed against the passenger seat.

How long would it be before she appeared? I cruised slowly to give her enough time, but there was no sign of her and soon I was pulling up outside the flat. Maybe she'd be waiting for me inside. I looked at my finger as I climbed the stairs. It hadn't bled; I'd cauterised it. I stuffed my hand in my back pocket to check on the map. It was still there. My finger scraped against denim, but I felt no pain.

The flat was empty but it didn't feel like mine any more. When I put the record on and turned the volume right up I felt a druggy mixture of euphoria and emptiness. My forehead itched. I wondered dully who else was involved. The girl couldn't have recorded, cut and pressed a record all on her own; she needed accomplices. Someone had to inhabit the streets on my map.

I looked at the thousands of records lining the walls. I had wasted so much time.

In the kitchen I switched the ring on full and watched it get hot. I could still hear the music swirling around me. My forehead was hurting, like scratched sunburn. Maybe I could burn up the pain. As I bent over the cooker I heard a car pull up outside.

I left the kitchen without switching off the cooker and looked out of the living room window. There was a black Mini parked in front of the Escort. I crossed to the door to leave and as I looked back for a moment before closing the door I felt a tug.

As I stepped into the street I felt a warm breeze and detected the faint odour of gas. The map was in my back pocket. I reached for the door handle on the Mini but the girl gunned the engine into life and moved forward several feet to dissuade me. I walked towards my own car, glancing in through the Mini's rear passenger window.

On the back seat lay a long knife.

I followed her in the Escort. She turned off my familiar route into the warren of semi-circular streets where I'd lost her the first time. She turned right again and drifted down to a set of lights which changed as she approached them. A left turn, more houses, and she pulled into a short gravelly drive, parking next to a big wire mesh gate. Beyond the fence were two huge gasholders. She unlocked the gate and started walking towards the nearest of the two.

It reared up before me, an awesome monster of overlapping curved metal plates. A telescopic spiral ready to expand or contract. It glowed in the moonlight, appearing to hover just above the ground like a ghostly carousel.

I followed the girl until she reached the base of the gasholder, the long knife sticking out of the back pocket of her jeans. She turned and looked back. The moon fell on her face. Her hair was swept back from her forehead which I now saw properly for the first time. She was the perfect synthesis of Siouxsie Sioux and Annie Risk, possessing the most beautiful face I had ever seen. My stomach went into a slow dive. I would have wept but for the detail on her forehead which, though I only caught the briefest of glimpses, chilled me.

She turned and vanished around the side of the gasholder.

I followed because it seemed to me that there was nothing else I could do. I went around the back of the huge structure but the girl had disappeared. I collapsed against the side and my cheek rested against the cool metal. I opened my arms to embrace the structure. Over my panting I listened for any sound of the girl – or of gas. But each was as deathly quiet as the other, if either was there at all.

Chapter Five

THE PROBLEM I had with my nocturnal adventure was that I didn't know how much of it I had dreamt and how much had really happened.

I had a burnt finger that remained sore for weeks and I still had the white label single which I played even though there was no music recorded on it. The hisses and ticks and booms could represent some kind of message but I had to find the key to unlock the code. I'd stick it on the turntable in the morning after waking up and it was a gentle start to the day, provided my downstairs neighbour wasn't working an early shift. I'd smoke a cigarette and lie there propped up against a couple of pillows trying to discern order from chaos. After a while I formed the impression that the sequence of sounds actually changed with each playing. Because I found this such an attractive idea I didn't check it by recording the single on tape and comparing the two – which would have been easy to do – in case I discovered I was wrong. I suppose this idea and act of self-denial were the first steps I took on my own initiative into fantasy. But almost certainly I wouldn't have taken them at all if it hadn't been for the girl in the Mini.

I started to think of her alternately as an imaginary siren and as a real woman who was in fact out there somewhere. And in both these roles she became my quarry. She could be a distraction from the elusive Annie Risk.

One night after shutting up the shop I drove around between King's Cross and the North Circular for two and a half hours, just cruising, looking for the girl. From the back she looked like millions of other girls so I was forever slowing down and rubbernecking. I was lucky not to get picked up by the police. Each time I sighted a black Mini down a side street I'd make a late turn and check it out.

Held up by roadworks on the A10 in between Tottenham and Wood Green I remembered something that made me realise I was probably wasting my time. Years ago in a Crouch End pub I'd sat mesmerised for half an hour by a girl drinking with another girl at a nearby table. When her friend accidentally knocked over the ashtray, the first girl and I had exchanged a look and she had smiled at me. I formulated a dozen chat-up lines but lacked the nerve to use any of them. She had dark brown hair tied back with a faded silk scarf and was wearing old jeans and a tan-coloured T-shirt that was cut pretty low for the time. When they got up to go I was looking at her and she smiled at me again. The smile was so friendly I felt certain she would have listened to me if I'd tried to strike up a last-minute conversation. All it needed was a remark about the pub or the warm weather but I dried and she walked out of my life. I followed her discreetly out of the pub and watched as she and her friend split and walked in separate directions. It was a Saturday lunchtime, the sun was beating down and this girl was right there. I'm not saying I'm a catch, but you know when someone's given you a look, and all I had to do was catch up with her, apologise for staring in the pub and see where it went from there. Instead I watched her wait at a bus stop, climb on board a W7 and disappear in the direction of Muswell Hill.

I went back every Saturday lunchtime for the next eight weeks but never saw her again.

As the lights changed to green and I slipped through the single lane section of the A10 I wondered if my search for the hybrid girl would end the same way. There were at least six million people crammed into the capital and I was hoping to catch sight of one of them. It doesn't matter that you can bump into one of your oldest friends on Neal Street when you haven't seen him for twenty years or that you can recognise the same complete stranger two days running in Tube stations at either end of the underground system – you never come across whoever it is you want to see, especially if you're out there looking for them.

I took a left and headed back towards home. It was dark now and I tried to concentrate on the road but I kept looking around at everything. I noticed a man who'd paused in the act of drawing his curtains together in a first floor flat above a bookmaker's. He was gazing at the horizon above the row of shops opposite.

I was growing tired of driving but snapped awake when I saw two great gasholders on my right. I checked the rearview mirror and slowed down. There was a turning into a gravel driveway which ended at a pair of wire-mesh gates. Slowly I swung around, turned in and scrunched to a halt on the gravel. When I switched off the engine I could hear my heart beating. For five minutes I didn't move from the car but just watched the gasholders for any sign of movement. There was a slight breeze which disturbed the tops of the trees but nothing else. I stepped out of the car and closed the door quietly, then approached the gates. When I'd been here with the girl she had used a key to unlock the padlock which now barred my way. But not for long. I climbed up the gate using the pointy toes of my cowboy boots to gain footholds in the wire mesh. I teetered at the top and dropped down in a crouch on the other side.

Unlike the last time, which had felt like a dream and may, for all I knew, even have been one, now I knew I was trespassing.

I looked around for any reaction to my break-in and once satisfied I was unobserved I moved off at a low run in the direction of the nearest gasholder. I'm not a small man and the noise generated by my progress was deafening: sticks, litter, gravel, puddles. My size elevens came into contact with every obstacle and I considered the wisdom of getting hold of a pair of trainers if this sort of thing was going to become a regular feature. I might still have stashed away somewhere the baseball boots I used for the courier job.

The gasholder blocked out the light. The street lighting, obscured by trees, was poor anyway. There were a couple of big floodlights on the other side of the gasholder but now I was in its shadow. I don't know what was scaring me more – the idea of getting caught or of finding the girl – but I could have done with a hot bath, a cold Sapporo and a neck rub. I went up to the base of the gasholder and reached out to touch it. My finger withdrew abruptly in a reflex reaction, though the metal wasn't hot. I had felt something, a slight jarring, maybe the displacement of gas inside. Now I pressed the flat of my palm against the metal wall and felt nothing apart from the ghost of that first reaction.

I laid my other hand on the metal and thought about how I was tapping into a system that ran the length and breadth of the country. Millions of feet of pipes carrying fuel from gasworks to homes and industry, hundreds of gasholders storing and supplying gas according to requirements, themselves literally rising and falling with demand.

Within half an hour I was back in the flat with a beer and a Chinese, watching ice-skating recorded a couple of nights earlier. I'd already started watching it the night before but I'd been so tired I'd fallen asleep. I'd kept waking myself up and managing to watch a minute or two at most and then my eyes had closed again. For some reason, even though it's a recording and you can watch it any time, you try to watch it all the way through, even when you're clearly too tired. You know you'd enjoy it more if you waited. But still you persist.

There was an Italian girl skating. Sveva Ricciardi. I remembered the name from the night before. She was putting together a fairly ordinary free programme, which I felt sure I'd seen the night before, when suddenly she jumped a quad. The commentator was as surprised as I was. 'It's a quad! Ricciardi jumped a quad!'

I moved to the edge of my seat.

The thing was, she hadn't done that the night before.

The obvious explanation was I'd slept through it the night before. But a small part of me felt sure

I'd been awake throughout her performance. I even remembered her score coming up at the end. A string of 5.8s and a 5.9 from the Austrian judge.

So I could have fallen asleep for a second. A microsleep. That's all it needed.

But the other thing that happened was that no sooner had she landed than the phone rang. I stretched and picked it up, said hello a couple of times but there was no one there. That was no coincidence. Or I was becoming paranoid, and I didn't buy that.

The Italian girl jumps a quad. The phone rings and there's no one there. Again.

I keyed in Annie Risk's number.

'Hello?' she said. I loved the way she said that.

'Hi. It's Carl. Listen, was that you? Did you just ring me?'

There was silence for a moment before she answered. 'What?' She said it wasn't her but we talked for a while. I said I hoped she didn't mind me ringing her this late and she said it was always a pleasure. I smiled at that and asked if I could go up and see her for the weekend, not expecting her to say yes. So I was gobsmacked when she said, 'Yes, OK. I'm not doing anything this weekend.'

'I'll come up on Saturday evening,' I said, aware I mustn't seem over-keen.

That was Wednesday night. The rest of the week passed at the speed of a man reading a book in a language that is not his own. I spent most of Thursday and Friday abstractedly dealing with customers while puzzling over a detail in *Un Régicide*. Boris discovers a gravestone for a student called Red. By this stage, Boris has already decided he is going to assassinate the King, for no other reason than that he doesn't like his smile. The inscription on Red's headstone reads *Ci-gît Red*. Here lies Red. It was one letter away from being an anagram of *régicide*. Why had the author settled for something that was almost an anagram but not quite? And how would a translator possibly render that in English? It wasn't my problem, of course, but it gnawed away at me.

Saturday came around and it too went slowly. I was left pretty much alone so I spent most of the day looking at the map. I wondered if it could turn out to be part of Manchester, but I'd checked the appropriate A–Z and ruled out that possibility. Nevertheless, like the Italian skater who jumped a quadruple salchow, the second time the tape was played maybe the streets on the map would insinuate themselves into Manchester in time for my visit. Reality was mutating.

As soon as it started getting towards five o'clock, I waited for a lull in customers and closed up early. I could have driven up but I chose to take the train because I was tired after a hard week. Running a record shop single-handed was no joke but it was beginning to feel like one.

I took my seat at Euston and settled down to enjoy the journey. I had a can of some inferior beer from the buffet and a packet of Camels, a seat at the front of the train, in a smoking carriage, naturally. I pulled down the little table on the back of the seat in front and spread out the map.

As the train rolled through the Midlands I watched the light get squeezed out of the sky by a bank of deep violet cloud in the west. I peered down single-track branch lines that peeled off from the mainline. Their secrets were kept safe by thick stands of trees and thorny bushes.

At one point the railway ran alongside a main road, then the two diverged and smaller roads passed underneath the tracks. The train flew past a depot with sidings where strings of freight trucks stood waiting. Two rows of shunters and larger diesels loomed. Because I rarely travelled by rail I was fascinated by the detail, by the intricacy of the network laid out over the whole country, a multiplicity of directions of travel, different routes to destinations; a world of possibilities.

In my life I got up and I went to work and sometimes I walked around the West End, drove around North London – a limited set of variables. The structure and scope of the rail system attracted me in the same way as the gas pipes. The depots were like gasholders. Maybe those trucks would sit there months; or maybe they'd get shunted into service tomorrow.

I was in awe of this vast network of communication that I had no part in, nor any real knowledge of. There were so many secrets, so many discoveries to be made.

I swigged back the rest of the lager, lit another cigarette and folded the map. The closer I got to Manchester the more excited I became.

Suddenly I felt a cool draught as if someone had left a door or a window open. But these new trains were hermetically sealed. I shivered and felt goose pimples rise on my arms. As I reached for my leather jacket and twisted to get my arm in it, I happened to look outside. It was quite dark now and I couldn't make out very much apart from trees and ditches and tangles of nettles and brambles. A branch line swung in from the left. I looked down it as the train sped past. The twin rails curved away into darkness.

Then I noticed something flashing. Two little things that flashed together like eyes. I wondered if they were my own eyes reflected in the window but pretty soon, as I shaded my view and concentrated, I realised that I was looking at a pair of eyes outside. They flashed in the light from the train carriage. What's more, they were keeping up with the train.

I cupped my hands either side of my face and stared back at the eyes.

I went cold. Then hot. And cold again as I started to sweat.

It was a dog running alongside the train, jumping as if it were all a game, but those eyes weren't playing. The beast was bounding along, leaping over bushes and piles of dumped sleepers, head twisting to the right so it could watch the train. I could see its strong white teeth as the loose flaps of skin around its mouth flew up and down. Thick strings of saliva trailed behind its head. It looked like a bull, eyes rolling, tossing its head one last time before goring its taunter. I briefly shuddered. Its pumping flanks were slick. It opened its mouth and showed an impressive set of teeth. Still it kept pace with the train. I looked around the carriage. There were only two other passengers, heads turned the other way as they stared into the darkness outside their side of the train.

I looked back, hoping that the creature would have disappeared, but it was still there, leaping at the glass and snapping its jaws. I found myself unable to look away, terrified that if I did the dog would somehow manage to get inside the train, either by leaping through an open window between carriages or by smashing a window with its skull – the thing looked hard enough. Now it actually began hitting the side of its head against the window, and the skull cracked like a fancy chocolate, smearing strawberry cream on the glass. I reacted – recoiled, yelped – but the other passengers continued to look out of their own windows. I started to question the reality of what was happening. The dog was doing things that shouldn't have been possible and whereas I liked that in an ice-skater or a singer I wasn't sure I was in favour of it for dogs. I'd always believed I'd rather submerge myself in a bath of spiders than meet a pit bull terrier down a dead end street.

It was hard to tell, because of the speed and the poor light, but I thought it was a pit bull that was beating its head against the window.

The train wasn't going very fast but neither was it crawling along. I was rocking forward on my seat willing it to go faster. The dog showed no signs of tiring. It thumped its head against the glass, working its jaws on the night air like scissors. The eyes were the worst because they were so blank, devoid of intelligence. I felt sucked into them. I had to get away; specifically, I had to go to the bathroom, in a hurry.

I locked the door behind me and for a moment felt more secure. I used the facilities and stood looking at my white face in the mirror.

But I'd been an idiot.

There was a thud on the outside of the frosted window. In the confined space it was deafening.

I'd been an idiot by not taking care to use the toilet on the other side of the train.

There was another solid thump and with an almost imperceptible bending inwards a fine map of cracks spread itself over the small square of glass. I watched it transfixed. With one final blast the window shattered, sharp triangles scattering over me and over the floor, and the dog's wicked, ugly head thrust through into the tiny cubicle.

I stood unable to move, a wave of revulsion sweeping through me. I watched the dog and the dog watched me. Then the head whipped from side to side catching the neck on jags of glass and spotting the floor with blood. Its eyes followed mine but I couldn't move. The dog lunged forward, cutting its throat more deeply, and snapped its stinking jaws at me. I felt its hot breath and sticky spittle on my face. The animal made another lunge forward, and its throat was opened so deeply by the glass that a jet of dark blood struck me in the chest. This seemed to set me free. I grabbed at the door handle and within seconds was reeling about the space between the carriages tearing at my formerly white cotton shirt – panicking, muttering, laughing, crying, all at the same time. After pulling the toilet door shut I'd been able to hear the blood drumming against the door.

Once I'd got rid of the shirt I pulled my leather jacket around me and sat hunched up, shivering in a corner by the door until the train pulled into Stockport. The two people who'd been sitting in my carriage and had remained oblivious to the dog's assault got off here without even glancing at me. They walked off towards the exit without a backward glance. Weird fuckers, I wanted to shout after them. What kind of twisted, secluded lives were they returning to? I pulled the door shut and wrapped my arms around my legs to try and control the shaking that had taken hold of my body.

*　　*　　*

I TOOK A cab from Piccadilly Station to Annie's place, which was a top floor flat in Mayfield Road, Whalley Range. As I stood waiting for her to come and answer the door, I looked across the main road to the mature trees of Alexandra Park. Just the other side of the park was Moss Side, and Maine Road football ground, home of my boyhood club, 'the only football team to come from Manchester', as the song went. The door opened and Annie looked at me shyly with her head on one side, then glanced down at the threadbare carpet and fidgeted.

'Aren't you going to ask me in?' I said, then followed her up the hallway.

'The neighbours are nice,' she said as we climbed the stairs. The building smelled faintly of laundry, alcohol and Indian food.

'Have you made me a curry?'

'I thought you might be hungry,' she said, leaning on the banister and looking down at me. I was still checking out the steel door to the flat below. 'They've been broken into six times.'

'Perhaps they should get a new door.' I suggested.

'They did,' she said.

'Yeah, I, er… Never mind.'

Annie's door was a sturdy wooden affair. 'Have you not been broken into?' I asked as she closed it behind me.

'Only once,' she said. 'They took my collection of coloured glass bottles. You know, they were just about the only things I cared about and they picked them out of everything else. Two thousand pound computer? No thanks, I'll just have these old blue bottles, they might fetch ten quid down Affleck's Palace. I couldn't believe it.'

'Seems weird,' I agreed. 'Are you sure it wasn't someone you know? I mean, it sounds like it might be a personal thing.'

She seemed to consider this and then asked, 'But who'd do a thing like that?'

'I don't know,' I said, 'a wronged boyfriend, someone you sacked or beat going for a job. The world's full of people with reason to want to hurt you.'

'Well, fuck me, I'm glad you came.'

'I didn't mean it like that. It's just, you can affect people's lives without meaning to and we never think about them coming back and saying, "Hey, I want to get my own back."'

She gave me an odd look and walked into the little kitchen.

I didn't know what had come over me to make me say such things. 'Hey, I'm sorry,' I said. 'I'm tired. The journey was… well, it was a journey.'

'Make yourself at home, Carl. Take your jacket off,' she shouted above the noise of the kettle and I realised I couldn't. I needed a shirt.

'What happened?' she asked, coming back into the main room and looking at me standing there like an extra from *Dawn of the Dead*.

'I had to throw my shirt away,' I said. 'I spilt something all over it.'

She gave me another odd look, which I added to my collection, but she did go and get me a shirt from her bedroom. 'It should be big enough,' she said as she passed it to me. 'It's one I use to sleep in.'

A momentary thrill. The thought of having her night shirt next to my skin. She went back into the kitchen and stirred the curry while I took my jacket off and put the shirt on. It was a long white T-shirt with the words Holiday Time stencilled on the left breast. It smelt of washing powder.

'Do you mind if I use the bathroom?' I asked.

'Help yourself.'

I locked myself in and let out a big sigh. It wouldn't do me any good to be so nervous but so far I was getting everything wrong. She was probably sorry she'd let me come. I looked at myself in the mirror. I'd got some colour back in my cheeks and I needed a shave. Obsessed with travelling light I hadn't brought anything except a toothbrush and my copy of *Un Régicide*.

The bathroom was painted blue with bits of mirrored glass and glazed tile stuck on the walls like a kind of mosaic. She had lots of Body Shop soaps – fruit and animal shapes – and a big bottle filled with tiny sea shells.

I splashed cold water on my face and dabbed myself dry with a big soft white towel. There was a peach-coloured bathrobe hanging on a hook on the back of the door. I buried my face in it to see if I could smell her. The trouble was, I hardly knew what she smelt like.

I used the toilet, washed my hands and laid my hand on the door handle.

Before the door opened I had a split-second vision of me opening the door and there being nothing there but utter darkness. No flat, no Annie Risk, just emptiness, cold and vast.

Then it was gone and I stepped into the hall. I smelt the curry.

'Nearly ready,' Annie shouted.

'OK,' I called, but I could still feel the chill.

We sat on big floor cushions in Annie's lounge to eat the curry. She'd produced a bottle of wine and I hoped I wasn't going to make any more stupid remarks. I told her it was great curry and she smiled, pouring more wine. I relaxed and the conversation flowed naturally. We accepted each other's childhood reminiscences as if they were precious stones that we turned over in our hands and polished and put away in a safe place. The clumsy line on which I'd started the evening was forgotten, at least by me. By midnight two empty wine bottles stood next to each other on the table. After Annie had opened a third, the conversation took a darker turn and we started talking about ghosts, fears, dreams. I asked Annie what she was scared of.

'Birds,' she said, playing with one of the wine bottle corks.

'Birds? Why?' I asked.

'For many years I didn't know. I was just scared of them. It was a phobia; it didn't need a reason.'

'Fair enough.'

'But then one day I was walking across the park.'

'Alexandra Park?'

She looked at me, slightly exasperated, as she continued to turn the cork over and over in her hand. 'Yeah, probably. But, you know, any park. It doesn't matter. Just – the park.'

'OK, sorry. Go on.' I smiled at her.

'I don't know where I was up to now.'

'You were walking across the park.'

'And there was this great big crow in front of me. Just ten or twelve feet away. Great big thing. And it opened its big black beak and came out with this awful, harsh, raucous cry.'

'Yeah, they can be pretty frightening, crows,' I said.

Annie threw the cork at me and I ducked.

'The point was – or is – I wasn't that bothered by it, but it made me realise what it was about most other birds that freaked me out.'

'Go on,' I said as she paused.

'It was the disconnect between what they look like and what they sound like.'

'What do you mean?' I asked, my hand brushing Annie's leg as I placed my wine glass on the floor.

'I mean they have these horrible little legs with claws for feet, tiny little cold, black eyes, and most importantly this hard, angular beak out of which, weirdly, comes this beautiful burbling song. It doesn't add up. It's all wrong. It's not for nothing that Hieronymus Bosch painted so many birds in his visions of hell. They're horrible, nasty, weird little things and I won't have them anywhere near me.'

'Wow,' I said. 'You really don't like birds, do you?'

'I really don't like birds.'

We sat in silence for a moment.

'The wine's all gone,' Annie said, at length, leaning back against a cushion. 'But I can offer you something from the liqueur trolley.' She was pointing to the corner by the window. There was a small table with short legs and on it stood a bottle of Cointreau and what looked like some foreign brandy. From where I was sitting and with a quart of wine inside me I was having trouble reading the menu. It crossed my mind that if these floor cushions were *not* intended as my bed for the night I might not be in the best condition to make the most of any opportunities arising. But Annie had drunk as much as I had and she was a lot smaller, so in fact I was impressed she could still string sentences together coherently. We had a plum brandy each and Annie said to me, 'How about you then? What are you scared of?'

'Dogs,' I said.

Chapter Six

WHEN I WAS doing the courier job I stayed on the road as much as I could and kept out of the office if at all possible. The Thin Controller had vertical pupils, small bumps on either side of his forehead and he never got up from behind his control desk. If you sat down on one of the orange plastic chairs facing the desk his big black dog was always lying under the desk stopping you seeing his cloven feet.

What I'm trying to say is he wasn't a very nice man and try as he might to conceal his infernal provenance – never letting you see him standing up; the dog hiding his feet – just about every courier on his books had a good idea where he came from.

He called you up all the time, interrupting just when you were dismounting or delivering at some uptight Mayfair address, where more often than not a sign was fixed to the wall advising couriers to keep the volume down. I actually quite enjoyed doing jobs in Mayfair and Knightsbridge. Middle-aged receptionists would rumple their silk blouses and crease their foreheads as they turned and frowned at my entrance. The helmet, the fingerless leather gloves and the shorts – I acquired some Lycra after a couple of weeks; Jaz helped me get kitted out – were regarded as threatening at many W1 addresses west of Regent Street.

It wasn't always possible to avoid the office, however. The Thin Controller made a point of calling you in every so often. There was never any good reason. He'd give you a job he could just as easily have given you over the radio. It seemed like he just wanted to keep an eye on you. He liked confrontation. I didn't. So I dreaded him calling me in. It wasn't just the Thin Controller I didn't like; there was his terrifying dog as well.

If I've given the impression the dog never left its lair under the Thin Controller's control desk, scratch that. As soon as I reached the top of the creaky old wooden stairs from the street the dog was barking like a bastard and bounding along the top landing to meet me. As far as it knew I could have been some suicidally depressed burglar come for the Fat Woman's petty cash box. I'm not saying it was a stupid dog; I think, like its master, it was in league with dark forces. Whenever the Thin Controller called me in I used to think maybe the dog would have recognised the scent of his owner's couriers by now. Ha!

Every time I mounted those stairs I did so with my heart in my mouth.

The morning in question was no exception. The step three from the top creaked like a Jeffrey Archer plot and the dog was upon me more like something out of a certain Conan Doyle mystery.

Whenever I'm called upon to explain my fear of dogs I tend to overreact and get all incredulous, wanting instead, demanding even, to know why *we* should trust *dogs*. They are, after all, animals. Beasts with too many teeth. They're carnivorous and have small brains. Is that a good combination? All that stuff about man's best friend is bollocks. Man's most likely betrayer more like. One man's friend, another man's killer.

They don't think or reason. It's not, *Shall I bite this little girl's face off or shan't I?* It's just, *Bite, bite, bite the fucking thing off.* Owners think their dogs understand them and the reverse is true. All the dog's doing is picking up on a few basic reactions to repeated cues. It knows how to get food out of you and how to avoid getting hit. That's not clever, it's just survival.

I see mums and dads – dads most of all – letting kids play around with the pit bull and I just want to fucking shoot them. The one good thing the Tories did was introduce legislation about dangerous dogs. Being idiots, though, they didn't go far enough.

So, I'm at the top of the stairs and the dog's about to have my testicles for lunch. The Thin Controller does fuck all and the Fat Woman, sitting in her tobacco-stained office, just farts. I always dealt with the dog in the same way: making an effort to control my bowels, I would raise my hands above my head and make all sorts of ridiculous noises to soothe the beast. These ploys felt about as useful as opening up an umbrella against a tsunami but somehow I manage to sidle along the landing to the Thin Controller's control room, whereupon the dog retreats to his position under the desk, because it remembers I mustn't see his master's feet or it'll get a beating.

The Thin Controller was in the middle of giving someone a hard time over the air. Alpha Two Six by the sound of it. 'When I give you two jobs you do them in the order I give them to you, Two Six, not in some strange order you invent yourself. What do you think this is, a fucking holiday camp?'

I sat down on one of the orange chairs. The dog growled softly. I didn't know what breed it was, or what combination of breeds. I just knew I didn't like it very much.

While waiting for the Thin Controller I did the one thing that annoyed him and which you could get away with. I lit up. For some reason it irritated the crap out of him when couriers smoked in his control room but since he smoked roll-ups constantly himself there wasn't much he could say. There was, of course, because he was hardly a reasonable man, but he never told you to put it out. He just grunted his disapproval and looked even more put out than usual. It was Jaz who told me about the cigarette smoking thing. In the same way I would pass it on to someone else in the unlikely event that I stuck around long enough to be anybody's mentor.

Several couriers, health and fitness fanatics all of them, actually took up smoking just to spite the Thin Controller. And not Silk Cut Mild either; they smoked Capstan Full Strength, Woodbines and foul-smelling Turkish brands.

I tried to flick my ash over the dog but its growls grew louder, so I abandoned that.

The Thin Controller finished moaning at Two Six and took his rolly from between his lips with yellow fingers. He always kept his headphones on when talking to you. They were cheap-looking grey flimsy things like we used to use for language work in school.

He grunted. He did that: he called you in then acted like *you* wanted to see him. I never bothered to play along.

'You called me in,' I said.

'Did I?'

Not worth answering.

He shuffled various papers around on his desk, pretending not to remember what he'd called me in for.

'Got a job for you.' The words slipped out of the corner of his mouth like slivers of unwanted food. His antennae eyebrows twitched.

'A job, is it?' I said flatly.

He screwed up his face and lit the blackened rolly which had gone out while he'd been sorting through his papers.

'Don't fuck about, Two Three. Just do the fucking job for me, will you.' He plucked the rolly from his mouth and set about trying to remove a shred of tobacco from his tongue by blowing and spitting. Under the desk the dog stirred and the headphones crackled. I could just hear the tinny voice calling in. 'Alpha One Eight.'

'Where are you, One Eight?' A beat, a drag and the metallic rustling of the courier's voice. 'What the fuck are you doing in Regent's Park? You're going to thirty-six from Covent Garden and you're in Regent's Park. What is going on, One Eight?'

He went on like this for a while and as he was still talking dug a docket out from under the messiest part of his desk and held it out for me to take. I was relieved to get out of there. I looked at the docket as I returned to my bike. The job was somewhere near the Barbican, between St Paul's and Old Street. Not that far from the office. I freewheeled down Pentonville Road and took a left.

A few minutes later I was going down a bus and cycle lane with a line of traffic stationary on my right and some fucking well-intentioned idiot left a gap in the queue and waved through a Vauxhall Astra that was aiming to cross from the other side of the road into a garage forecourt on my side. But the driver didn't look out for me. I could almost forgive that. It was the twat in the Golf who waved her through I soon wanted to have buried alive.

So the Astra crossed my path – nice and slowly as well, that was the essential comedy touch; if she'd been doing more than ten miles an hour I'd have missed her – and I braked but there wasn't much point. My front wheel smacked straight into the rear door and then I was flying. It must have been an impressive sight for all the motorists sitting in their cars with nowhere to go as my body described a parabola in the air above the Astra and landed with a sickening *crump* in the bus lane just beyond the car.

I lay still and in total silence for a few moments not knowing if I could move, not daring to try in case it was bad news. Then the spell was broken as the driver of the Astra came running and crouched down beside me. 'I'm so sorry,' she was saying. 'I'm so sorry. Are you all right? He waved me on. I thought it was clear.'

I sympathised. She hadn't wanted to hurt anyone. Obviously she should have looked instead of relying on the wave. It was the man who waved I wanted to have a stern word with, but the traffic was moving again. Which was more than I was.

'Are you all right?' The woman was frightened she'd done terrible damage. At this stage I still didn't know. I was just lying there sort of enjoying the attention and the luxury of being able to lie flat in the middle of the road. 'Please say something,' the woman implored.

'OK,' I said, deciding it was time to see what the score was, and I started to feel my way back into my body. It was all there, as far as I could tell, and in one piece.

No dogs yet, but stay with it. I'll come to the dogs.

Soon I was getting to my feet and the woman was helping to dust me down. I probably ended up cleaner than before. She went and looked at my bike before I did. She was gone a while, around the other side of the car. Meanwhile everyone was just driving past, slowing down to look for blood on the road. When she came back I was lighting a cigarette. I was shaking like fuck but had been remarkably lucky to have sustained only grazed ankles and an extremely sore back and shoulders.

'The news is not good,' she said, wearing a very worried expression. 'I'm very sorry. It was my fault and I'll pay.'

'Don't worry.' I tried to reassure her. 'No bones broken, I don't think, and I'm not leaking smoke anywhere.'

She laughed nervously and we both went to take a look at my bike. She had been understating it really. The bike was completely fucked.

'I've no idea what bikes cost,' the woman said, producing a chequebook and pen. 'If this isn't enough I'll write my name and address on the back, just let me know what else I owe you.'

I was a bit dazed at this point and didn't look at the amount. The poor woman was muttering away to herself about having to go. I dragged my bike onto the garage forecourt she'd been trying to get to and then she was in her car burning rubber. I sat down on the little fence at the front of the garage, lit a cigarette and looked at the cheque for the first time. Two hundred pounds. To me that was a fortune and would have bought eight bikes the equal of mine. I suddenly felt quite lightheaded and started daydreaming about spending all that cash. I was brought back down to earth by the Thin Controller's nasal voice crackling over the radio.

'Alpha Two Three… Alpha Two Three. Where are you, Two Three?'

'I had an accident, control.'

'What about the job, Two Three?'

What a cunt. No *How are you? Are you hurt? Was it serious?* None of that. For all he knew I could be in casualty with only my voice still functional and the nurses were only waiting for him to call before unplugging the machines.

'I've got to do something about the bike, try and get it fixed up,' I said, surveying the wreckage in front of me.

'Will you be able to do it?'

'Probably. The wheels aren't too good. A couple of new wheels and a bit of work and it should be OK.'

'The job, Two Three.' His voice had risen an octave. I could almost smell his dog and his disgusting roll-up cigarettes. 'Will you be able to do the job?'

As I say, what a cunt.

I wanted to tell him to roll the job up tight and stick it up his arse and I'd help if he was having difficulty.

'The job will get done but it may take a while to fix the bike,' I said through clenched teeth.

'Call me when you've done the job, Two Three.'

I lit another cigarette and kicked my bike. Then I remembered the cheque and smiled. Two hundred quid. I hoped there'd come a day when I'd demand a good deal more to cheat death and be completely humiliated in the space of ten minutes, but the state of my finances at that time meant it was a pretty good deal.

I left the pile of scrap where it was and walked the remaining mile and a half to the job address. I often asked myself later why I bothered to complete the job, given that I'd decided after picking myself up off the road – even before seeing the state of my bike – that I would ride no more jobs for the Thin Controller.

There's a part of me that doesn't like to leave loose ends. I find it hard to walk out of bad films and I never leave a football match until the final whistle even if my team are three goals down and leaving five minutes before time would get me home an hour earlier. I like to see things resolved. It sort of all ties in with my love of maps and my search, years later, for the city on my map.

It was painful to walk for the first quarter of a mile but then I seemed to loosen up and I knew how best to place my feet to minimise the jarring effect.

I headed vaguely south. I had my A–Z in the big fluorescent bag along with the radio and the job itself. Sometimes I wondered what was in the envelopes and packages I delivered. I liked the mystery and the sense of bringing people together, becoming a conduit for their communications. This job was a stiff-backed envelope, A4 size, bearing an address label and the words, handwritten in ballpoint, 'By hand'. Despite my natural curiosity I had never been tempted to open any of the jobs.

The sun had sunk behind the old warehouses on the other side of the street. I wondered what I might do next. The idea of telling the Thin Controller I was no longer going to work for him frightened me a little. It wouldn't have been so bad if I could have just called him up and told him, but I had to return the bag and the radio, and I had to get paid for my last week.

Eventually I reached the street, without the aid of the map, and crossed over to the odd numbers, looking for number 23. At first there didn't seem to be one; it was a short street and the numbers only went up to 15. Then I noticed an alley down by the side of number 15. I turned down it and the alley opened out into a narrow road with old derelict properties on either side. They seemed to have been workshops and light manufacturing units. There were also occasional doorways that could have led to flats. Most of the jobs I did were delivering to businesses but very occasionally I'd get one to a residential address. There were no numbers on the doors and the street had not been given a name unless it was a continuation of the first street. Down near the bottom on the left hand side was an archway with the number 23 hand-painted on the wall at waist height. I passed under the archway into a courtyard scattered with household rubbish and black binliners ready to burst. All I wanted was a door with a letter box. I wasn't sure I would bother waiting for a signature this time. I was feeling nervous, though I couldn't account for it.

I heard a high-pitched keening noise like a circular saw coming from somewhere inside the building that abutted the courtyard on two sides. I saw a doorway but there was no door to speak of and certainly no letter box. A few bits of wood hanging on a rusty hinge wasn't enough for me. A job worth doing and all that. I stepped inside and immediately felt the temperature drop. The walls wept foul-smelling moisture. Boards creaked under my feet and I heard noise coming from somewhere ahead of me, the same high-pitched sound again and the murmur of men talking in loud voices behind closed doors. I should have left the job on the floor and retraced my steps but something drew me on. I wanted to know what was going on. I stepped forward, taking care over the placing of my big feet. The building smelt of grease and sewage. I opened a door at the far side of the room and found a corridor that stretched ahead twenty yards. It was very cold and water dripped from pipes that ran along the ceiling, forming puddles on the sunken concrete floor. I felt completely alone, as if no one could see me, no one knew where I was, not even the Thin Controller, who'd sent me there. It was something to do with the cold of the place and the sense of utter neglect. I could still hear the men's voices but something gave me the idea they'd reached wherever they were by some different entrance. I hurried to the end of the corridor and turned left into a disused office. Old telephones sat like fat spiders on desks thick with dust and fur. Cobwebs darkened every corner and I heard something scuttling behind the rusty filing cabinet. There was a louder noise though, coming from the far side of the room, which made the hair rise on the back of my neck. I reached a door and peered through the dirty circle of glass fitted at its centre. Beyond was a sort of galleried section with a wooden rail only fragments of which were still supported by splintered uprights. About eight feet below, at least a dozen men stood around a circular pit in which two dogs were fighting, yelping and snapping at each other as the spectators goaded them on.

My instinct for flight was countered by a compulsion to watch.

The two dogs – pit bull terriers – moved around the ring as they eyed each other and lunged forward, snapping their jaws. They were like boxers, but there was no referee, just a bloodthirsty crowd. The speed with which they darted at each other and withdrew increased as the sweat trickled down the back of my neck. With one attack the brown dog managed to fix its jaws onto the side of the black dog's head. The black dog jerked its head this way and that until there was blood spotting the floor of the pit and the brown dog let go. Black instantly leapt on Brown and sank its teeth into the back of Brown's neck. Brown tried to shake off the other dog and was successful but Black had torn away a chunk of hair and skin. Blood flowed from the wound. The men cheered and punched fists. As each dog launched fresh attacks I realised the men were split in their allegiance. Some were shouting, 'Come on, Griff!' while the others yelled, 'At him, Storm!'

Hair, skin, gobbets of flesh, streams of blood flew from the skirmish as the speed and ferocity increased and the men watching became more and more excited. I felt sick but couldn't stop watching. The dogs became ever more vicious, the fight clearly intended to last until one of them was killed. Soon, to me, they became a blur, a nightmarish slurry of spitting bleeding dog-flesh spinning around and around the ring. I imagined that if I approached I would be able to dip my hand into the flux. The air seemed charged with possibilities, as if the dogs were actually changing and I could change with them. At that moment the dream of escaping the humdrum seemed the reality. Mesmerised by the now golden flux of the fighting dogs, I fell against the door. The men turned and saw me through the glass, and suddenly there were dogs – other dogs – coming for me. I heard their feet clattering on a set of stairs and their mad barking echoing off the walls all around me. I sprang back from the door and looked around quickly to see if I could tell which direction they were coming from.

Within seconds they appeared in the doorway through which I had come. These dogs were fresh. They had mayhem in their eyes. I had the impression that they hesitated before leaping at me from the doorway as if savouring the moment before the kill, but it could just have been my mind playing tricks, like when you're in the car that spins out of control and you have that moment of utter passivity and sense of inevitability. They moved in slow motion, allowing me to see every minute detail of their bodies. A pit bull terrier can pull ninety times its own weight. It's bred for fighting and it never gives up, not even to save itself. This is what makes it so deadly. And there were two of them coming straight at me. One went for my hand, the other my leg.

Chapter Seven

LIGHT HAD CREPT into the sky outside the window behind Annie's head while I'd been talking. The birds had started to sing. I'd gone beyond tiredness and Annie also seemed wide awake. I lit a cigarette and noticed Annie looking at my hands.

'It healed,' I said.

'What about your leg?' she asked.

'There's a scar. It's not too bad. I walked with a limp for a while, a real limp.' Even if I'd wanted to get a new bike and carry on cycling I wouldn't have been able to. 'So you see why I'm frightened of dogs?'

'What about guide dogs? Guide dogs are OK, aren't they?'

My real problem was with the so-called dangerous dogs, those bred for fighting and kept by sociopaths, but it extended naturally to include all other dogs. 'Still not keen,' I said.

'So what happened after they attacked you? Did you manage to get away?'

'Jaz saved me.'

Jaz had heard that last exchange between me and the Thin Controller and had gone out of his way to see if he could catch up with me before I delivered the job. He was going to help me fix the bike or give me a ride, or just do the job for me while I fixed the bike. As it was, he caught up with me just as the dogs were released and he used an iron bar to beat them off me. He probably saved my life but Jaz being Jaz he shrugged it off when I was recuperating in his flat later.

Annie suggested we have a coffee and she went off to make it. Our heads were full of that spangly brightness morning brings after a sleepless night. A coffee would calm us both down. I knew I would probably crash at some point during the day. Gone were the days when I could stay up all night and not suffer for it. Jaz and I had gone to a couple of all-nighters at the Scala in King's Cross but we were younger then and our bodies could take it.

After coffee Annie and I went for a walk across Alexandra Park into Moss Side and past Manchester City's ground at Maine Road. It was warm and overcast.

'Probably be a storm later,' I said and Annie nodded. Apart from that we didn't say much. But it was OK: there was no need to talk and no awkwardness in the silence. I felt I could almost have taken hold of her hand and she would have been glad. Occasionally the sun broke cover and splashed an end terrace or a back entry. Fast food containers scuttled around and around in shop doorways as a breeze got up. Sheets of newsprint rose up like kites and grit got into our eyes. Annie stopped and bowed her head.

'Something in my eye,' she muttered. 'Will you see if you can see it?' She tilted her head back and pulled the skin away from beneath her eye. I'm squeamish about eyes and I almost had to cry off, but I steeled myself and peered into the red insides of Annie's eye.

There was a tiny particle.

'Found it,' I said.

'Will you get it out for me?'

I had to see what I could do – she was in discomfort – so I took a clean tissue from my jeans pocket and folded it to get a stiff corner. I asked Annie to lick this so it would be less abrasive and very gingerly I lowered it to the inside rim of her eye where the little black mote was lurking. I felt queasy dipping into such delicate matter. I didn't like to see the hems along which the body could come undone. But with careful probing I caught the piece of grit on the end of my tissue and removed it. I showed it to Annie and she looked at it – holding my hand to steady it – and said, 'God, it felt like a rock.' I was sorry when she took her hand away.

We wound up in Rusholme and had lunch in one of the dozens of Indian restaurants that lined both sides of the road.

'How do you decide which one to go in?' I asked as our jug of Cobra beer arrived and I poured us both a glass.

'Easy,' she said, breaking a poppadom. 'I go in a different one each time.'

'Then you know which ones are no good and you avoid them next time around?'

'Nice idea,' she said, dipping popadum into chutney, 'but I always forget.'

We ate in silence for a while. There were so many things I wanted to say to her that I couldn't think how to start.

'Food's good,' I said when the main course had arrived.

'What's your favourite kind of food?' she asked.

'Oh, Indian, I think, or Chinese. There's this great Chinese right underneath my flat. You must come to

London again and try it.' I cringed inwardly. It was like, *Do you want to come up for a coffee?*

Annie smiled.

'What's yours?' I asked.

Because she had a mouthful of aloo gobi she pointed at her plate with her fork. 'This stuff,' she said after a moment. 'Indian vegetarian food. It's bloody great.'

'Ask me what my favourite word is,' I said.

'What's your favourite word?'

'Yearning. And my least favourite is inevitable.'

'Clearly,' she said, 'for what they mean rather than the sound of them.'

'I had a friend who said life *is* yearning. I didn't know what he meant at the time but I think I do now.'

'How come?'

I told her about the map. That wasn't the whole story, of course, about yearning, but it had become a quest that seemed to represent the way I felt about life.

I told her how I'd found it and verified that the streets belonged to none of the major towns in the country. I tried to explain how I'd decided the map represented a real place despite this, and how I was determined to find it. She listened closely and at no point did she attempt to rationalise the whole business.

'How will you find it?' she asked as the waiter hovered. We ordered gulab jamun.

'There are clues,' I said. 'All around us.' I realised this was the point at which she could either accept what I was saying and go with it or decide I was paranoid and announce she would never see me again.

'What sort of clues?'

'People must know about this place,' I said. 'Someone lost the map in the first place. So sometimes

I see people talking and something about the way they look makes me think they know.' I spooned a suet ball into my mouth. 'Have you never sat on your own somewhere and watched other people?' I continued. 'And seen two people sharing a joke or talking with serious looks on their faces and wanted – and I mean *really* wanted – to know what they're on about?'

'Of course.'

'Well, that's all I'm saying. That's the reality. The rest is metaphor, if you like. It's all about knowing what they know, slipping into their lives, almost *being* another person. Have you ever thought how strange it would be to *be* another person?'

She nodded again, frowning.

'That's all it is,' I said. 'Knowing what others know. We're all too isolated. It'd be great to know everything.'

'I don't know. I like the mystery.'

'So do I, though. That's what it's all about. Mystery. Not knowing. Wanting to find out. Mystery is a transient thing on its way to knowledge. It's like a sheet that you're trying to get at to pull aside. Look,' I said with a sudden movement backwards. I reached into my back pocket. 'This is it. This is the map.' I unfolded it and spread it out on the cloth. 'What do you think?'

I watched Annie looking at the map, followed her eyes as she examined the streets, the squares, the boulevards.

'It exists somewhere,' I said, then the waiter came back and we ordered coffees.

*   *   *

WE WALKED SLOWLY back to Annie's place, taking short cuts down back entries.

'I like these places,' I said. 'They're like secret passages.'

Annie laughed. 'We're trespassing really,' she said. 'It's only the kids who use them. Grown-ups use the streets. It's a sort of unwritten law. I use them sometimes because they remind me of being a kid. I like that.'

'Me too,' I said. 'It's like me and my map. Your childhood is a strange place, like the city in the map. And it's good, isn't it? It's good to go back there. Or make it feel like you've gone back.'

'Do you want to play Scrabble when we get back?' she asked out of the blue.

I gave her a look.

'I used to play it when I was a kid,' she offered with a smile.

'In that case, yes.' I said. 'I like Scrabble.'

I did like Scrabble but I never won.

Annie made a pot of tea and we sat on the floor in her living room.

I got rubbish letters to start but got rid of them in a couple of goes and after ten minutes I had five letters of a seven-letter word. The word was ADVANCE and I needed only the last two letters. In their place I had a useless K and I. So for the next quarter of an hour I scored in single figures, placing only one tile each go while I hoped to pick up the C and the E. Annie laughed at my piddling scores as she raced ahead. I got the E but it took ages to get the C and of course once I'd got the word the board was almost full and there was nowhere to put it. Chasing a fifty-point bonus had lost me the game, as it almost always did.

Game over, we sat back against her huge cushions and our sleepless night caught up with us. Within seconds I was drifting off, dimly aware of Annie's head resting nearby. I felt very peaceful, extremely relaxed.

We weren't actually asleep that long, a couple of hours at the most. Annie stirred first and her movement woke me. Her head was inches from mine and I could see her eyes moving and a wisp of hair that had fallen across her mouth rising and falling.

'Sleep well?' I said.

'Mmm.'

I took hold of her hand, which was lying curled up on the cushion next to her head, and she squeezed my hand firmly. Then she turned and was facing me and I looked at her for a moment before leaning forward and kissing her.

We made love slowly, undressing gradually and spending a lot of time just holding on to each other and either just watching or kissing each other softly.

For a short time I felt slightly detached, observing myself while my mind raced off on its own, recording the various sensations, the emotions. Annie's body welcomed me like a warm scented bath, and as I immersed myself, the foamy water stroked every inch of my skin.

Later we lay in a cushioned embrace whispering silly things to each other. Reluctantly I reached my hand under the cushions, looking for my watch. It was time to go if I was going to catch the last train back to London.

'You can stay if you want,' Annie said.

'Better not,' I said. I wanted to but I'd made the mistake before of too much too soon. When my mother warned me in my teens that to go too far with a girl too quickly would spoil the relationship in the long run I had never believed her. But experience had taught me she had been right. She usually was.

I got dressed and went to the bathroom. When I came out Annie was walking across the hallway towards me, her hair in her eyes and orange street lighting from the windows catching her hip and the side of her body. My mouth dried. I felt a rush of blood and had to be strong-willed as I enfolded her in my long arms that for once didn't feel as awkward as the unfastened arms of a straightjacket. I kissed her on top of her head and she caught hold of a handful of my hair and gave it a little tug.

'Are you sure you don't want to stay?' She pressed close to me.

'Better not,' said a part of me that believed in walking away from piles of presents wrapped in shiny paper with the name Carl written on each one. Another part of me was all for staying and never going anywhere ever again. But I knew we'd stand a better chance if I left now and came back again soon.

'I'll see you soon,' I said, kissing her on the lips. 'Thanks for everything. I've had… you know what kind of time I've had.'

As she opened the door for me Annie said softly, 'Have you got your map?' I patted the back pocket of my jeans and smiled. 'Good,' she said, 'you don't want to get lost.' And she kissed me again lightly and locked the door after me.

I SAT AND waited on the platform at Piccadilly and smoked a cigarette. I walked along to the end of the platform and looked out at all the lines going off into the darkness. I felt a lot closer now after my weekend with Annie, particularly after the last couple of hours. I was beginning to find my way. As I stared into the darkness I saw at its very heart a light, at first just a pinprick, emerging and expanding. Excitement grew in me as the light got bigger and bigger. I waited for it.

Sitting in the first carriage as the train headed back down south through the night, I looked out of the window. No terror dogs tonight; only a row of terraced houses – beyond Stockport but not yet in Macclesfield – all in darkness except for one bright top-floor window washed yellow like a painting with a figure in the centre of the frame waving his arm at the train.

He knows, I thought. He knows.

THE FOLLOWING WEEK was one of the best. I had the memory of the weekend just gone and the promise of the next. Annie and I spoke on the phone during the day on Monday and arranged that I would go up again and this time I would take my car so that if we wanted we could drive out somewhere for the day.

I enjoyed working, talking to customers, dealing with enquiries. I embarked on a new filing system for the jazz section. The old system split everyone up into male singers, big bands, modern jazz, trad and so on. But that was no good for people like Mose Allison – sometimes he sang, sometimes he just played – or Courtney Pine, who switched musical styles like Imelda Marcos tried on shoes. So I changed it to a straight alphabetical thing and for someone like, say, John Lee Hooker I put a card in the pop/rock section saying SEE JAZZ.

Which reminded me. I hadn't seen the old bastard for a while, so I gave him a ring and nipped around to Bethnal Green after work on Wednesday. I told him about Annie and he was very enthusiastic. I said nothing about the map. I still wasn't sure how he'd react and, anyway, by now I liked the idea of it being mine and Annie's secret.

The gasholders across the canal shone like two huge polished copper saucepans. An open window admitted smells of rotting fruit and engine oil rising from the scummy olive-green canal. Jaz offered me a beer but I said no and asked him if he had any mineral water instead. He looked at me like I'd asked for giraffe essence.

'Course I haven't got any fucking mineral water, you ponce,' he said. 'But I can lower a bucket into the canal if you like.'

He went off to the kitchen muttering about fucking mineral water and came back with two cold bottles of Budvar.

'Christ,' he said, 'you only went to fucking Manchester. Not exactly Paris, is it?'

I laughed.

'The pictures look good,' I said. He'd framed several of his urban landscapes and hung them on the walls.

'You haven't fucking looked at them,' he said from the depths of his armchair.

So I went slowly around the room like it was an art gallery. Jaz was talented. And obsessed. OK, the light was different in each photograph and even the location changed, but the subject was the same: England as Post-Industrial Wasteland.

'Like I said,' passing behind his chair, 'the pictures look good.' I grabbed hold of his shoulders from behind. He squirmed and I clapped him on the arm and let go.

'You're in a funny mood,' he observed.

'I'm looking forward to the weekend. Cigarette?'

I delved into my boot and chucked him a Camel. We smoked and I got two more beers from the fridge. The light disappeared from the sky and the gasholders hovered in shadow. 'They're bigger than last time I was here,' I said.

'They're fuller. When the gas gets pumped in they rise.'

'I know,' I said, stubbing out my butt in the big black ashtray on the floor by Jaz's chair. 'I'd best be off if I'm going to make the Hong Kong Garden before it closes.'

'Have a good weekend,' Jaz said.

The remaining three days went quickly and on Saturday I locked up early, leaving a note on the door saying early closure was due to British Summer Time. That should have confused a few people. In August. I drove north on the M1. The good thing about not starting your weekend until Saturday evening is that the motorway is empty, because everyone else started theirs twenty-four hours earlier. Still, quality not quantity.

When I got to Manchester, around 9.30pm, we went out for a drink at the Princess. It was excellent to see Annie, but I was exhausted after the drive up and as soon as we got back to her flat I passed out and was no good for anything until morning when I was woken by sunlight slanting through the bedroom window. I watched Annie sleep for a while then slipped out of bed without waking her and went to fix some breakfast. I even popped out for a paper.

We had breakfast and read the paper in bed for an hour, then drove to Formby. It was a beautiful day and we parked a couple of miles from the dunes. The marram grass found its way up the legs of

Annie's 501s but I was wearing my boots outside my jeans so I was OK. I offered to carry her and she told me to fuck off so I pushed her down a dune. She rolled over a couple of times and shouted 'You bastard!' loud enough to confuse the ships heading for Liverpool docks. I gallumphed down the side of the dune, sand getting in over the top of my boots, and when I was level with her she grabbed hold of my ankle and pulled me over.

We spent the afternoon enjoying the privacy of a hollow between three high dunes. The sun caressed our bodies. I had to cover up after half an hour as I was starting to turn pink. My long hair is only dyed black from a rather disappointing mousey colour. Late in the afternoon with the gentle roll of the breakers in our ears and the wind whistling through the marram grass we made love. The sand was a problem but it made it more fun. The second time, Annie came quite quickly and I couldn't. 'It doesn't matter,' she said, and for once I believed it.

Back at Annie's flat, we made love in bed for the first time and it seemed to me as the sweat poured off me and Annie's back arched higher that what we were attempting lay in the same realm as the quintuple ice jump and the coloratura soprano's super A. We wanted to do it no matter how unlikely we were to succeed because we felt sure we could. Mainly it was about wanting it, yearning for it. Every muscle in our bodies ached for it.

We didn't quite make it, though we got pretty close, floating in the outermost rings of its ripple effect. At the centre, I believed, was something unworldly – two people reaching their climax together and becoming undone as individuals, being remade as a single organism just for a split second of real time, but in that state of flux it would last for an eternity.

It was like the dogs in the old factory. Their fighting became so wild and uninhibited they entered the flux. Which could explain why, although they revolted and terrified me, I had been attracted to the golden spinning ring of dog flesh.

In the early hours I slipped out of the flat while Annie slept. She had known I would be going but I left her a note anyway. In it I told her I thought I might have fallen in love with her.

I headed south through Sale and Altrincham to connect with the M6 at Lymm. I felt fine though I knew that tiredness could creep up on me at the most inconvenient times and none could be more inconvenient than when driving on the motorway. Determined not to give sleep a chance I switched on the radio and messed around with the dial until I heard something with enough balls to keep me awake. In this instance it was a jazz programme and the record playing was Cat Anderson or some other trumpeter who could blow like Anderson. Whoever he was he certainly could play and he wasn't scared of high notes. I thought of Annie lying in bed, then of the two of us reaching our peak. We had cleared the bed in our excitement. The duvet was on the floor, the pillows thrown against the walls, as we circled each other, first with me above, then Annie, then me again and so on. For over an hour.

Cat Anderson was really going for it now, his notes sharp squeals in the confined space of the car. I turned the volume up and again it was me and Annie on the bed almost dancing around each other in our rapture. Anderson went higher and higher. I saw the golden ring of the dog fight. The starry delirium as Annie and I plunged deeper and deeper into each other. The trumpet was suddenly playing notes a trumpet shouldn't play. The trumpet player had done it. He'd gone through the ceiling. He held the note. Surely it was the highest I'd ever heard. The sort of sound we're not supposed to be able to hear, never mind get out of a trumpet. Too high-pitched for the human ear. Annie and me coming within a split second of each other. Just beginning to go, to lose it. The dogs whirling around and around and around. The trumpet's triple G.

The glass in the speedometer dial smashed. In a shower of blue sparks the radio blew and possibly one of the tyres also. The engine died. I broke out in a sweat. There were cars coming up fast behind me.

Part Two

'The key words are love, power and fear and all the songs are concerned with one of those ruling forces. The stunning opening piece, "Fear", sets scenes and scopes. It takes the form of a conversation – between "them" and "us" – about ruling force: "they" ask us what runs this place. Three forces are offered. Power. Love. Finally and realistically: Fear…

'After "Fear" there are two equally wrenching songs of *fear* – "From the Heart" and the closing "Prelude". These songs are desperate searches: rebellion in a vacuum? The songs are laid out and structured to imply a spiral: upwards and onwards, round and around, constant movement.'

Paul Morley, 'Fear! Anger! Power! Love! – and More Mancunian Melodies', *NME*

Chapter Eight

LUCK HAD NOT deserted me. The cars behind all had room to overtake and I drifted unsteadily to the left, my legs shaking with shock, and the car came to a dead stop in the gravel on the hard shoulder. I sat very still waiting for whatever was going to happen next. Because that's how it felt: I was a passive figure in a drama unfolding in front of me. I could only watch. But now I sat in a silence broken only by the occasional car bowling down the middle lane. Each time one went past, the Escort rocked. It was almost comforting.

After a while I tried the ignition. Nothing. Radio: dead. Lights: no response. The car had died and I had been lucky not to have done.

I got out and had a look at the car. One of the tyres was shredded. Otherwise there were no obvious signs of what had caused its demise. I reached into my boot for my cigarettes. I had more than half a pack. I lit one and drew in a lungful. Mixed with the sharp night air it tasted good. My legs were still trembling but the smoke was counteracting the bitter taste of fear in my mouth.

I smoked the cigarette and walked around for a few minutes before I felt able to get back on top of things. I opened the door and got my jacket from the back seat, then took the keys, locked the car and set off looking for an emergency telephone.

There were two quite close but neither of them worked. I even crossed the motorway to one on the other side but that didn't work either. My breakdown membership had lapsed but I had to get off the motorway somehow.

I walked further on and spotted a sign up ahead. It was only small and no higher than my waist, so probably was not an exit road. The sign grew larger but only slowly. Two more minutes and I was able to read it. 'Work vehicles only', it said, and just beyond it there was a sharp turning to the left, a single track road which led off into the darkness. I had to try it. My road atlas was still lying open on the floor at home so I had no idea how far it would be to the next proper exit. There were no major well-lit areas visible from where I was. This service road offered a glimmer of hope, at least. There were even a couple of lights winking in the velvety distance that could be workmen's trailers or farmhouses.

I left the motorway and walked into the darkness.

The narrow road seemed to go on for a long way, petering out as a track. There was no light other than that of the cold stars and I stumbled over a cattle grid. The further I walked the more my mind drifted. The problem of the car became less serious even though there was no sign as yet of how I was going to get out of this mess. I just kept walking with the single-minded purpose – or abstraction – of the very drunk.

The track rose slightly and seemed to go over a small bridge. I stopped at the highest point and went to the edge of the track to see if I could hear or see

anything. But it was all too silent and dark. There
was a smell but I couldn't place it, so I walked on.
I lit a cigarette. If I'd been tired earlier I felt wide
awake now but increasingly it seemed that things like
tiredness and knackered-out cars just didn't matter a
great deal any more. I walked on, my boots making
a humble *clump, clump* sound soon swallowed by
the fields on either side of the road.

I saw a light in the distance, possibly one of
those that I'd seen from the motorway. As I got
closer, though, it became obvious it was neither a
constructors' yard nor a farm building. It was bigger
than both and, in this setting, far stranger. I thought
I knew what it was but had to wait until I was closer
to be sure.

Flat as a pancake and as big as half a football pitch
– floodlit from eight points – here, in front of me,
was an open-air ice rink. I gazed at it in wonder.
Quite apart from any other consideration I wanted
to know how it stayed frozen in the open air in the
middle of summer. But the longer I stood and watched
the sparkle of the light shimmering on the surface of
the ice, the less its incongruity seemed to matter. I
lit another cigarette and as I was bending down to
slip the pack back down the side of my boot a skater
slid onto the ice. She wore a black outfit, a tight top
with a loose flapping skirt that glittered with tiny
flints of mirrored glass. I watched, entranced, as she
completed a circuit of the rink, presumably unaware
of my presence, her hair and her skirt trailing out
behind. The ice shone so brightly under the lights it
seemed almost to hover above the ground. I saw the
girl bend at the knee as she came down towards the
corner nearest to me and I knew she was going to
jump. My heart beat faster. And when she jumped

and twisted and kept on twisting before touching the ice my stomach flipped, my head spun and I was back in bed with Annie Risk, the trumpeter hitting his triple G. The skater was already at the far end of the ice and jumping again. There may not have been any commentary to help me but I was pretty sure she had just executed a quadruple salchow. She went into a steps sequence for all the world as if she were practising for a competition and then slipped into a spin that far surpassed anything I'd seen. She spun so fast she lost all solid form and I drew a sharp little breath when I realised she had risen at least six inches above the ice. Then she came out of the spin like wine being poured from a carafe and skated away to the far side again where she jumped another quad and drifted off the ice, melting into the darkness.

I stood watching the ice for two or three minutes hoping she might come back. I knew I hadn't imagined her: I could still make out her signature scratched on the ice's glittering page. Only when I turned away and felt the movement of air on my face did I realise the effect her display had worked on me. There were cold tear tracks down both my cheeks.

I walked on, and once the ice had been swallowed up by the darkness behind me I began to wonder if I'd hallucinated the whole episode.

In the darkness on both sides of the track I became aware that things were starting to change. Where there had been only trees and grass there now stood sturdier shapes. It was too dark to see what they were but soon I noticed the irregular echo of my footsteps which told me the track was edged intermittently by buildings. In the distance I saw light and in a few minutes I was walking under streetlamps that shed a diluted milky light over the disused workshops and factories lining my route. Soon, I hoped, I would find a phone.

But even after passing the openings to several side roads I still hadn't seen a kiosk. I passed one or two beaten-up vehicles, trucks that appeared to have been abandoned. Apart from these dubious clues I saw no signs of life and so just kept on walking.

I appeared to be heading into town. God knew what town: some grim Midlands industrial community. The frequency of side streets increased and my track had widened to two lanes with a white line down the middle – a road, then. I saw a few old cars dotted about and the factories were soon replaced by four-storey blocks of flats. There were occasional shops all shuttered and padlocked. The street had that strange, alienating feel common to all dark streets. In the full light of morning – if I hadn't managed to find a garage or a phone by then – it would all look quite different.

The streets changed again and now looked like the area around Annie's flat. I could have been wandering about lost in Moss Side. Long low rows of terraces and back entries, whatever they called them around here. I was surprised to find myself in such a heavily built-up area when there had been no sign of it from the motorway.

But still there were no phones. I turned off my straight route once I formed the impression I was heading away from the centre of whatever town this was. I wasn't even sure I would be able to find my way back to the motorway.

I felt a tickly sensation at the back of my skull even before I heard the muted rumble of the engines and then the sensation spread to the base of my spine. My mouth went dry. I looked about for a hiding place then stopped myself: what was I scared of? If there were vehicles approaching could I not stop them and ask for help? On a rational level there should have been nothing to fear, so why did I seem to have three small rats chasing one another's tails in my stomach? The rumble got louder; I heard a gear change. I thought they were still several streets away, whoever they were, but my mistake became clear as two police cars turned the corner at the far end of the street and headed slowly in my direction. They were perhaps a hundred yards away. I flattened myself against the wall but they would still be able to see me.

I should have been able to ask them for help but I was frightened. There was no one else about, the air seemed unnaturally still, and the police cars proceeded so slowly it could only mean they were on the lookout for something or someone. My head was buzzing now and beads of sweat had sprung up along my hairline. I didn't know which way to turn, where I could hide. The cars rolled closer.

Another movement caught my attention. Out of the corner of my eye I noticed a man beckoning to me from a car parked in a side street. The engine was running. To get to him meant crossing the road in full view of the police cars. If they happened to be looking to the front their beams would probably just pick me out and I sensed that might mean trouble. I didn't think it was a brilliant idea, to get into a car with a complete stranger, but if I stayed put I'd almost certainly get picked up by the police and I had no idea what trouble that might lead to.

I crouched low and ran across the road, ducked into the side street and jumped into the waiting car, which took off immediately, throwing me back in my seat.

'What you doing out?' the driver asked, his tone incredulous. He was short and dark, wearing a woollen hat pulled down over his forehead and a black bomber jacket. His gloved hands gripped the wheel. I was too shocked to know what to say to him. 'What you doing out on the streets at night? You want to get shot? You must be mad.'

'My car broke down,' I said.

'What do you mean, your car broke down? You shouldn't have been out in it. Asking for trouble. Where did it break down?' As he fired these questions at me he steered the black car around the most unlikely bends and corners at speeds that seemed out of all proportion, but he drove with such confidence that I trusted him. Even when we appeared to be heading straight for a lamppost it always side-stepped the car neatly at the last second.

'On the motorway,' I said.

'On the motorway?' he exclaimed. 'What motorway?'

Fear spread through my insides like smoke. 'Where are you taking me?'

'To a safe house,' he said, leaning into another ninety-degree corner and tearing out of it like a bishop out of a brothel. I decided to shut up and let the man drive. Watching the side streets flash past I got the impression we were skirting the city centre. If any police cars came into view at the end of any street my driver quickly re-routed us down some unlikely alley, hurtling into the darkness without headlamps. There were no other cars or pedestrians about though I did glimpse dark blurs of movement around the base of buildings, which could have been dogs. At major intersections there were statues mounted on plinths. As far as I could make out in the dark they were all the same man: a tall, broad-shouldered figure wearing either a trench coat or a double-breasted suit with a trilby-style hat. Something about his deep-set eyes and square jaw unsettled me. This was no ordinary Midlands town. Frightened and confused, I began to find myself short of breath.

In a street of anonymous uniform terraced houses the driver emergency-stopped outside a derelict-looking building.

'Safe house,' he said. 'Go in and wait. Someone will come.' As I was hesitating, he explained, 'Wait for someone to come. You might have to wait till dawn but they'll come.'

'Who are you?' I asked him.

'I'm Giff. If you need me, don't ask.'

I turned and got out of the car.

'Get some sleep,' he suggested, and with that he accelerated out of the gutter, the passenger door flapping wildly until he took the corner on two wheels and it slammed shut. Feeling exposed, I tried the door of the house. It was locked. Panic threatened to rise in me. There was no access down the side of the house and the windows in the front room were all closed. I wondered about the houses on either side but Giff had been specific. Not knowing what else to do I took off my leather jacket and balled it around my fist and punched a hole in one of the windows.

I jumped in and landed in a crouch. Looking around to get my bearings I wondered if I should answer the phone. Then, seconds after, I couldn't work out why I'd thought that. To start with, the phone wasn't even ringing.

I had a look around. The house was in slightly better shape than its exterior had suggested;

nevertheless, the carpets were threadbare, the balustrades rickety, and there was a fine film of dust stretched over all the surfaces. The floorboards upstairs sagged and groaned under my weight. I placed my boots as lightly as possible. When I was satisfied all the rooms were empty I lit a cigarette and watched the street from an upstairs window. It was dark and quiet. Only the stars allowed me to see fifty yards down the street where I noticed a curious stone or concrete seat fashioned into the wall at an intersection. It was too high up to have been designed for passers-by, so I wondered what its function might be. For all I knew, it could have been neo-utilitarian sculpture.

I could hear dogs barking somewhere off to the right but the house itself remained quiet. When my legs got too tired to allow me to continue standing by the window I went and sat against the wall. I was close enough to the window to hear if anyone came and I was determined not to fall asleep. Cupping my hand to shield the flame I lit another cigarette and waited some more. I concentrated hard on the environment of the house, listening for any sounds at all, and watched the sky for a change in the light.

WHEN I WAS very young, maybe eight or nine, I came into the house one day to feed the hamster that we kept in a cage in a corner of the dining room.

My father was out at work and my mother was weeding in the back garden. I got down on my hands and knees in front of the cage and peered in. Sometimes, when he wasn't running in his wheel, Cassidy would lie down behind his water bottle at the back of the cage. At first I couldn't see him at all and I crawled closer to the cage. He was indeed lying at the back but something about him didn't look quite right. There was something different about his tiny bulk; his coat was dull. I opened the cage door and gingerly reached my hand in – Cassidy had bitten my mother and me a couple of times. He didn't move when I touched him lightly with one finger so I prodded him harder to wake him up. He rolled slightly, whereas I would have expected him to spring to life and turn quickly to see what was going on. I pushed him again and he just slid across the straw on the bottom of his cage.

My breath was coming quite fast and I realised I was burning red. Guiltily I looked around to see if by chance my mother had come in and was standing watching. But I was alone.

I picked up the hamster and lifted it out of the cage. It lay in my hand without moving. Normally you would feel its tension as it prepared to jump out of your hands or you would just feel its small, warm pulse beating in your palm. Instead it was just there. I rolled it from one hand to the other to see if I could wake it up. I realised I was grinning nervously and immediately wiped the expression off my face in case someone came in. Turning Cassidy over I looked closely at *his* face. It looked no different. His eyelids were closed as if he were asleep. I threw his little body up in the air several times and caught it then I put it back in the cage in the same position I had found it.

It was my first experience not only of death, but of the death of something I cared about. And for a while my reaction to it worried me. Why had I thrown it up in the air like a toy? Why had I preferred to leave it for someone else to discover?

* * *

IN THAT DARK upstairs room I drifted in and out of sleep, half-dreaming about my mother and the pleasure she used to get from weeding and gardening before it became an obsession and her only comfort. As she knelt at the edge of the lawn and rooted through the catmint and rhododendrons for stray grass seedlings and twists of bindweed I would watch from my bedroom window, pictures of footballers and pop stars decorating the wall behind me, and listen to the dogs barking in next door's garden. Except that the neighbours didn't have a dog.

I suddenly came wide awake and pricked my ears.

Dogs.

I heard them quite clearly and it wasn't just a matter of a couple of strays picking over rubble. These were the real thing. I jumped up and ran quietly to the window. The street was empty and light had begun to creep into the sky. I could hear the dogs around the back of the house, maybe not in the garden or yard of the house itself, but pretty fucking close. Too close for my liking. My blind trust in Giff was beginning to look a bit previous. I heard more low growling and scurrying of feet and needed no further encouragement. I crossed the tiny landing and stepped into the back bedroom. Its boards, too, were bare and I had to walk lightly to avoid making a noise. I crept to the window and hugged the wall next to it as I looked outside. My heart raced. Half a dozen strong black dogs came running up the back entry. They stopped outside the gate that led to the little yard directly below my window. With saliva spraying from their snapping jaws they jumped at the gate and thumped it with their thick skulls. They looked like the dog I'd seen from the train. It wouldn't take a pack of pit bulls very long to break down a simple wooden gate.

Another figure appeared. This was a heavily built man walking with a stoop. I couldn't make out his features in the darkness. He strode purposefully through the dogs – which parted without a whimper – and rattled the gate.

I was down the stairs in two seconds flat, careless of the racket my boots were making, and at the front door with my hand on the latch as the gate to the back yard gave way. I heard the dogs growl like a single organism as they leapt across the yard and straight into the back door of the house. It splintered on impact. Fuck it, I thought, and yanked open the front door.

The street was deserted.

As I ran I heard the dogs break into the back of the house behind me and I ran faster, wishing I'd thought to shut the front door behind me – every second was vital and there was no point me making it easier for them.

I ran as fast as I could, my boots clumping and jacket buckles jangling. I was hardly inconspicuous. The identical streets closed around me as if they were folding me in. I saw no sign of human activity but I sensed the dogs couldn't be far behind. I dived down a back entry and almost slipped on the cobbles and long wet grass. Turning right at the end I ran along the entry, the darkened backs of houses and their yards lining both sides of the path. At the end I emerged into a street lit by a meagre handful of dirty orange lights. I heard the car too late. It screeched around the corner and caught me in its full beam. I leapt back into the entry but a man jumped out of the passenger door and seized me before I'd got ten yards. Exceptionally strong, he hauled me back to the car and pushed me in through the rear door. We sped off and I picked myself up off the floor, recognising the black beanie of Giff bobbing above the back of the driver's seat. There was another man in the car, in the front passenger seat, and he turned to look at me. He was unshaven and had staring bright blue werewolf eyes, but his gaze was neither hostile not self-congratulatory. Only later would I realise what it was.

'That safe house wasn't safe,' Giff said.

'No shit.'

'It was safe a week ago. They're tightening up.'

I just sat there and waited, resigned, wondering who 'they' were and whose side Giff and Wolf were really on.

We pulled up outside a large heavy tenement block with external spidery fire escapes and very few windows that were still intact.

'Take him in,' Giff said to Wolf. 'I'll park round the back. And,' he placed his left hand on the other man's forearm, 'be gentle. We're supposed to be looking after him.'

I wished someone would address me instead of just speaking about me but Wolf was already tugging at my arm.

'OK, OK,' I said. 'I can manage.' I got out of the car and allowed the staring man to lead me into the tenement building. He glanced about nervously. I shivered as I smelt animals.

'What is it?'

It was the first time I'd heard him speak and it was a shock. He spoke with a quiet, educated voice which belied the wild look in his eyes.

'Animals,' I said. 'There are animals here.'

'Only rats,' he said. 'No dogs. No problem. Let's go.'

As we made our way up the creaking wooden stairs I heard Giff enter the building from the back and run to catch up with us.

'Don't,' snapped Wolf as I gripped the banister rail. I let go and he demonstrated by kicking out one of the spindles. The rotten length of wood turned somersaults in the air as it fell down the stairwell and clattered among the rubbish piled up in the foyer. Giff had caught up with us.

'Trying to bring the house down, are you?' he snarled at Wolf, who looked wounded. 'Let's get him inside quickly.' He meant me.

Wolf kicked open a door and there was a desperate flurry of activity inside. As we stepped into the room a man pointed a gun in our direction.

'Put it away, Professor,' Giff growled.

'You should have warned me. There were clearly three of you and I was expecting two.' The Professor was a tall, thin man with small rimless glasses that flashed as his head moved. As we went further inside I noticed the Professor staring at me like Wolf had done. He didn't let up until I had sat down on a battered old sofa covered with an off-white sheet. The Professor turned to Giff and said, 'Is this really him?'

Giff just grunted and the Professor lost his shyness, looking directly at me and asking, 'Is it really you? Was it you?'

I shrugged. This game was beginning to annoy me. I was tired and disorientated. Whoever I was supposed to be I was not sure I wanted the attention.

'I'm tired,' I said. 'I need rest.'

The Professor nodded and Wolf looked at Giff, who wiped a hand over his head to remove his black woollen beanie. I kicked off my boots and swung my legs up on the sofa. No longer bothered about what I should and shouldn't do, I really did need some sleep.

'You're safe here,' I heard Giff saying in a low voice as I stretched out on the sofa and closed my eyes. 'At least for a couple of days.'

I had no intention of sticking around that long and it was only as I was drifting off to sleep that I remembered the map in my back pocket. Too tired to reach for it, I spread it out in my head and sought to trace a circuitous route out of this dark place back to my car on the hard shoulder of the motorway.

As my conscious mind gradually closed down, however, the streets changed to those of my childhood: the interlocking rows of terraced houses around the corner from our street of semis, the back entries smelling of rotten fruit and old prams, the 16-year-old girls who walked along the street across the top of the entry with their short pleated skirts and bouncing red hair, the tiny sky-blue invalid carriages parked outside the prefabs near the railway line, the dogs that snatched free ad-filled newspapers out of my hand as I stuck them through letter boxes, our flame-haired window cleaner Jim and his sleepy wife in her half-undone dressing gown, the advancing shadow of the only neighbourhood boy who was bigger than me.

Stamford Jackson was an unusually fair-minded bully. Most adolescent terrorists would pick on the smallest kids around and make their lives miserable but Stamford Jackson chose me, the second tallest child in all those roads off Heath Street, perhaps because he worked out that if he established his dominance over a big kid it would prove just how powerful he was to everyone else. Maybe he could sense also that I was a pushover – literally: the first time he hit me I fell and bruised my ankle on the cobbles down one of the entries at the top of Heath Street.

The first time I saw Stamford Jackson was on my paper round. I was nearing the end, having done Jim's house – and failed to spot his half-naked wife through the curtains – and Sally Darke's. I'd seen Jim's wife once when I'd happened to look in through their front window and she'd been bending down to pick something up and her dressing gown had fallen open. She hadn't seen me but I had of course looked in their window every week after that and never seen her again. Sally Darke was a girl who'd been a couple of years above me at primary school and who had once said something vaguely encouraging to me like 'Lanky bastard'. Occasionally I saw her going in or coming out of her house and she sometimes flicked Vs at me and skipped past. I knew that if I said anything to her it would ruin it and she'd never look at me again. If I didn't speak to her I could maintain the fantasy of a perfect relationship.

I'd also done all the houses that had dogs – I knew them well – and I'd not had my hand bitten off. At the top of Heath Street there was a funny little road that had a cul-de-sac going off it and that's where Stamford Jackson lived. I didn't know this at the time though I had heard of him from the kids I used to hang around with. I was delivering to the houses in the cul-de-sac, running up and down the paths and banging the gates, and I came to a house that had its front door standing open. The hallway was spectacularly untidy and dirty and I stood and looked at it in amazement. I didn't know how anyone could live in such filth. Half-empty tins of Dulux Non-Drip Gloss, upended coffee mugs, an ashtray with about two thousand cigarette ends in it, a pair of dark blue underpants with dirty white piping, a copy of the *Sun* open at page three and some obscenity scrawled across it in red ballpoint, a crushed box of Mr Kipling's Bakewell Tarts and a Wilbur Smith paperback with the spine broken in several places. And this was just the hall.

What I didn't know was that I was being watched from the front room bay window. A sharp rap on the glass made me jump. There was a grey-haired old man wearing a vest that swelled over his belt, and his son who towered over him.

'What are you fucking looking at, you nosy cunt?' the old man snapped.

'Fuck off,' the boy added.

'Just delivering a paper,' I said.

The old man came striding into the hall at full tilt. He grabbed the paper from the floor and threw it at me.

'Take your fucking paper. We don't want it, nancy boy. *Fuck off.*' He was practically screaming at me. The huge boy, still standing in the bay window, was grinning. I turned and ran as far as the embankment to the new road that had turned this street into a cul-de-sac. I was shaking. I ran up the embankment and crossed the new road which, unfinished, was still a sea of mud, thinking that I would finish the papers later.

I hung around on the footbridge over the railway line for twenty minutes, watching the electric trains scuttling into the station, their pantographs sparking against the wires. I thought of my father saying there was no romance left in the railways since the end of the steam era. I didn't agree but I understood why he said it: he missed the trains he'd watched in his youth, whereas these electrics and the diesels that pulled freight wagons through Skelton Junction and over Broadheath were all I'd ever known and I couldn't imagine them ever changing. I tried to imagine standing on the bridge and being enveloped by a cloud of steam from a locomotive passing underneath.

When I thought it was safe I crept back to the cul-de-sac to complete my paper round.

Stamford Jackson was waiting for me in the entry two doors down from his house.

'What you fucking doing here, kid?' he barked. 'My dad told you, we don't want your fucking paper.'

I started to back off but he said, 'Come here.'

I should probably have done anything but obey his command. I should have flicked him the Vs and legged it. But I went to him. I didn't know why. Simply because he told me to, perhaps. I walked into the entry, my long legs wobbly on the slippery cobbles, and he took one swing at me, hitting the side of my head. I went straight down with a deafening ringing in my ears and feeling sudden pain from my ankle.

'Don't fuck about round here,' he said while deciding whether to kick me as I lay on the ground catching my breath. After a while he wandered off and I felt my head gingerly to see if it was cut. My fingers came away red and I felt tears pushing at the corners of my eyes. I hated bleeding.

When I'd limped home, I told my mother I'd slipped taking a short cut down one of the entries. She fussed over me, which was nice, and I didn't feel guilty till I had to lie again about the newspapers. 'They were over,' I said of the dozen or so papers still in the bag.

'You don't often have any over,' she said as she pressed a cold butter knife to the rapidly swelling cut on the side of my head.

When my father came home, huge and reassuring in his dark double-breasted suit which smelt of damp wool and cigars, it was my mother who told him what had happened. He looked at me in a particular way he had when he knew there was more going on than he was being told. It was a very direct look which only lasted a moment and I never knew if my mother saw or understood it. I didn't want to tell them about Stamford Jackson for shame. I felt that my father would have expected me to put up a fight. He would have done so in a similar situation. He'd worked down the pit and in the docks before getting where he was today, which was in fact a bit of a mystery to me. I knew it had something to do with a club and a group of other men. Sometimes they came around and sat in front of the fire in the front room in a huddle of smoke and steaming cloth and I heard them using phrases like 'venture capital' and 'fixed assets'. If my mother saw me listening she shooed me away and closed the lounge door quietly before retreating to the kitchen where she would be preparing a huge plate of sandwiches. The front room smelt for days afterwards. I used to sit in there for as long as possible, thinking it was good training for being grown up.

The next time Stamford Jackson saw me I was coming home from school. It was a cold day and he was wearing a big grey duffel coat. I was just wearing my blazer because I didn't have a big coat and I didn't like wearing my anorak to school. For some reason I laughed at Stamford Jackson's duffel coat. I may have made some remark as well because he was on me in seconds, punching my ears and frog-marching me down the street away from my house. I saw where he was leading me: at the end of the street near the railway was a patch of wet cement. I struggled to get free but there was no question of me having any control. He took me right to the edge of the cement and, grabbing my blazer collar, sent me sprawling in it.

He laughed as I flailed about trying to stand up, but eventually walked away back the way he'd brought me.

I couldn't say I'd accidentally fallen in wet cement so I told my father when I got in that Stamford Jackson had done it. Calmly he got his hat from the hook by the door and left the house. I ran through to the front room so I could watch him walk up the street, his trilby making his head appear to tilt to one side as it always did. He walked in a relaxed way, not too fast, but he seemed to know exactly where he was going and what he was going to do.

I never found out what he did do. All I know is that Stamford Jackson never bothered me again. Occasionally I'd see him at the end of a street or down an entry but he'd always be the first to look away. My school uniform had to be replaced but I was never blamed or made to contribute to the cost.

Chapter Nine

WHEN I WOKE up, the Professor and Wolf were in the room with me, both fast asleep, and there was no sign of Giff. Whatever strange place it was I'd fetched up in, I thought I should take full advantage of their lapse in vigilance. Carrying my jacket and boots in one hand I tiptoed to the door. There was an awkward moment when the door seemed to be locked, but it was just stiff. I worked it loose very slowly and carefully and only pulled it to behind me. I didn't put my boots on until I had reached the ground floor.

My watch had stopped but I could see light streaming in through the cracks in the door to the street. There had been no windows in the room I'd slept in and I wasn't sure what to expect from outside. I think I imagined the streets awash with light but as empty as the night before so when I pulled open the door and stepped out I got a shock.

It was like penetrating a stream of energy. Like Oxford Street at lunch time. For a couple of minutes I allowed myself to be carried along with the flow and before I knew it I was half a mile from Giff's safe house. Even if I went back I wouldn't know which was the right door. I had burned my boats but that was fine because Giff and his colleagues were mad and I had to get back to my car. Annie might have been trying to ring me at the flat. She could be worrying about me. I wanted to let her know I was all right.

I drew back from the procession of folk and rested my back against an official-looking building. A steady stream of people entered the building by a set of double doors on the corner and as many left at an exit ten yards further along. Those leaving carried a small, regular parcel wrapped in brown paper. I wondered what it might contain. On the side was stencilled a capital letter M.

They generally looked slightly different to the people I was used to having around me in London or Manchester. Their features were recognisably European, possibly British, but there was something different about their look: clothes, hair, shoes, bags. The ensemble was all wrong. They looked a bit like the confused people we saw emerging from behind the Berlin Wall or scrambling aboard ferries to Brindisi when the communist governments toppled, as if they'd had a stab at copying western fashions but had followed a bunch of style magazines that were at least ten years out of date. In fact, they looked like they lived in another country – one that had little or no contact with where I was trying to get back to.

I noticed a few suspicious glances coming my way and realised I was standing out – in my white leather jacket, tight jeans and butterfly boots.

I looked around for the nearest side street. Fifty yards away. Head down I covered some ground and slipped out of sight. The crowd continued to press past at the top of the street. On a corner opposite was one of the inset stone bench seats I'd seen the night before. Sitting on it was a man in early middle-age wearing a tight-fitting shiny black suit. He was watching intently the people who passed by under his perch. As I watched, two policemen approached him leading a third man through the stream of passers-by. There was a brief exchange. I noticed with horror that whenever the suspect tried to speak up he was beaten on the legs by one of the two policemen with a stick like the fat end of a billiard cue. The man on the chair eventually made a gesture with his right arm, laying it across his own chest then pointing at the head of the suspect who had started to struggle. A mask of fear had settled on his face. Passers-by looked down at the pavement and hurried on. The policemen led the man away, one either side, and they turned into another street where I saw a black van waiting. The back doors were opened from the inside and the man was bundled in. His face pressed up against the glass as the van drove away.

The two policemen re-emerged from the street and melted back into the throng. I turned and walked in the opposite direction down my side street, away from the crowds. Turning right I saw people again at the end of the street and headed for them. At least I would be well ahead of the two policemen. Before the intersection I stopped and took out my map. I was well acquainted with its boulevards and grids of streets but had seen nothing so far that enabled me to orientate myself. Even if I were to, though, I knew the map would only represent a fraction of the city – or of the City, as I now came to think of it. I slipped into the crowd, slouching in an effort to blend in.

I looked around and accidentally caught the eye of a judge at the next corner. Behind his head was a street name – Great North Road – which I remembered from the map so I dropped my eyes and shuffled past as part of the general tide of wretched humanity. I felt the judge's eyes burning holes in the back of my head but when I had put enough distance between us that I felt half safe again I ducked into a doorway and took the map from my back pocket. I found Great North Road at the left of my map and worked out which way I was going. Then I reasoned that as I had been travelling south on the motorway and had found the City by wandering down a service road on the left-hand side of the road I had to go west in order to get back to the car. The Great North Road forked off the map near the top left-hand corner and there was no sign of any motorway or major road to the left of it.

I didn't dare ask anybody if they knew where the motorway was. Giff had been quite clear: there was no motorway. There was, of course, there must have been, but these people didn't know about it. I stepped back into the main street and set off in the other direction, heading north-west. For the first time I looked properly at the shops lining the route. They were drab and anonymous, named only after what they sold: SHOES, FASHION, IRONMONGERY, BOOKS. Displays were rudimentary and unenticing: windows full of dead flies and wasps, the odd badly dressed dummy, mismatched pairs of cheaply made shoes.

I turned my attention to the road. There were two steady streams of cars and trucks and I wondered if I would perhaps be better off in a car. I looked around but couldn't see any cabs. What would I have said to the driver? Just drive up here for a bit so I can see if it leads to the motorway. He would have said what motorway and I would have been heading straight back into trouble.

I walked up the Great North Road as unobtrusively as possible, feeling I ought to do something about my appearance but reluctant to do so as it would be like admitting I was stuck here for longer than I wanted to be. People brushed by on both sides, many carrying their brown paper packages stencilled with the letter M. Soon – when the pavement began to empty as they turned off into old, greasy-looking side streets – I realised no one was talking. In place of a buzz of conversation there was only a shuffle of feet, the slap of leather on slabs and cobbles. Had the police and street-corner judges cowed the people so much they were too afraid to speak? What did they have to hide?

I neared a kiosk selling newspapers, tobacco and confectionery. Some of the remaining pedestrians stopped to make silent exchanges with the vendor, an old grey man with heavy glasses. Crumpled old notes passed between them and the old man folded them into his pocket, handing out coins from his other pocket, taken seemingly at random. No one inspected their change. They just tucked their paper under a free arm or dropped a packet of cigarettes into a shopping bag. The kiosk looked like a stand in a railway station but more old-fashioned, with a timbered, lean-to, almost unfinished look about it. I tried to peep around the back to see if it was only half-finished but a small crowd pressed close to me and to avoid drawing their attention I was forced to move on. As I passed by, I read the blurred billboards that proclaimed: NEW LEADS IN HUNT FOR REGICIDE.

A police car growled past and I looked the other way, wishing I could have gone back for a newspaper, but caution made me carry on walking.

Since entering the outskirts the night before when I'd seen the ice-skater perform her impossible jumps I'd seen nothing else to suggest this was the city of my dreams. The dogs, the police presence, the general level of paranoia and this apparent hunt for some king killer suggested something quite different. I didn't want to think about it.

I concentrated on finding the motorway. I'd left the map now and as I walked further north-west I was becoming increasingly isolated. If a police car came by they'd be sure to pick me up. There were fewer shops, and gaps had started to appear between buildings. I looked down the side streets on my left but always at the bottom there was just another street of redbrick terraces running across. I heard a car with an ominous, low, rumbling engine and slipped through the first shop doorway I came to.

There was a sound, which was oddly familiar, and it was only when I took in my surroundings that I recognised it as the empty hiss of a runout groove. I was in a record shop. The smell of old much-thumbed sleeves washed over me. There were racks around the walls holding stacks of LPs, and a free-standing unit in the centre of the small, musty shop. At the far side was the counter and an old-fashioned till. Behind the counter was a door that was ajar but there was no one tending the shop. I was the only customer. Faint noises came from the half-open doorway. I also heard the police car cruise past the shop but instead of heading straight back outside I turned to one of the racks and flicked through the sleeves. They were all blank. I selected one at random and withdrew the contents. The transparent paper in the centre crinkled as I slid the record itself from the yellowed inner sleeve. The black vinyl shone like my father's shoes and when I looked close I could see a tracery of small scratches and insignificant scuff marks like those he had always tried to hide by slapping on Cherry Blossom Shoe Polish and brushing until he could see his face in the shoe.

I wondered what the record was. The label, like the sleeve, was blank. Over the loudspeakers I could still hear the stylus bumping around the runout groove of whatever record had been playing. I made my way over to the counter and looked around for the turntable. It was on a ledge below the counter and my heart stopped when I saw the record was only halfway through. The noise I was hearing had been recorded. I remembered the white label I'd dreamt the Siouxsie lookalike had brought me and I felt my stomach muscles contract. Then I heard something that made me shiver: a high-pitched squealing sound accompanied by the drumming of running feet. It was coming from the half-open doorway.

As I ducked under the counter and stepped through the doorway I slipped back twenty years.

I was coming downstairs first thing in the morning. My father was out doing some strange shift work. My mother was getting dressed upstairs and above the tinkle of her jewellery and the rustle of Radio Two on her transistor I could hear the pitter-pat of scampering feet and the squeal of the fast turning wheel. I trailed my fingers against the raised knobbly paint patterns – like purple waves breaking on some dream shore – on the hall wall and turned into the dining room. The squealing got louder, the feet ran faster. I went and crouched down in the corner and watched our second hamster as he ran on and on against the gravity which meant he would never climb to the top of his wheel but would be condemned forever to run on the spot. I knelt down in front of the cage and watched him run. His little black eyes seemed to register the futility of the effort and yet he carried on running, even despite my close attention. If anything he started to run faster.

At the end of the short passage behind the shop I stepped into a semi-dark dusty room. There was some machine cranking away in the far corner that was responsible for the squealing and drumming I had heard. Straight ahead of me was another doorway which led to an uncarpeted staircase and to the back door. Through the glass in this I could see that evening was coming on. The sky was turning red. The machine drummed on. I realised there was a familiar smell that reminded me of some place but I couldn't think where. I had started to sweat. I could still hear the record playing from the shop – even though the machine's drumming noise was getting louder – as if someone had turned up the volume. A shadow extended down the old wooden stairs. I retreated into the shadows of the room, imagining angry shopkeepers coming at me from both directions. After all, I was trespassing. The shadow lengthened on the stairs and I took another step back and bumped into the pounding, shrieking machine. I caught my hand in something and felt a sudden sharp pain. I looked at my hand. The end of the short third finger of my left hand was burnt black and the pain quickly receded as the finger went numb.

Then I realised what the smell was – I remembered the toilet cubicle on the train and the dog that smashed its head through the window. I spun around and saw my 'machine' clearly for the first time. It was a large running wheel constructed out of two bicycle wheels spinning on an axis. The diameter of the wheel was increased by wooden extensions and the perimeters were two four-foot-wide hoops of beaten metal. Wooden slats were affixed between the two metal hoops, creating a wheel which spun around the central axis.

Running inside the wheel was a dark mottled pit bull terrier, its eyes flashing, ropes of saliva flying from its hanging jaw. It was staring at me as it ran, its nailed feet hammering on the wooden slats. The bicycle wheels squealed. The dog ran. I couldn't move.

Someone appeared in the doorway, having come down the stairs.

It was a girl in a dark, sliver-flecked skating dress.

'This way,' she hissed at me. 'Quickly.' She nodded towards the passage that led to the shop and even this close to the dog I could hear the dull booms and ghostly clicks of the endless 'groove' music.

I moved towards the girl, noticing that the hairs on my arms were standing on end and my legs felt weak. As I got closer I could see her long black hair shining in the yellowish light from the shop. Was she the girl from my dream? Or was she the skater I'd seen on the night I'd entered the City? I didn't trust her. I didn't trust my eyes. She wasn't real. I darted back into the passage towards the shop.

I barged into the shop just as two figures entered from the street.

'Fuck,' I said as I took in their appearance and turned back to the passage. But already they were coming for me. Stooped, twisted, black-haired bodies but with unmistakably human features, they covered the distance between the door and the counter in a heartbeat. I slammed the passage door after me and raced for the back door, which the dark-haired girl was holding open for me. As I fled across the space of the back room I heard the dog, no longer running in its wheel, give a powerful tug on its chain leash. It could smell my fear and it wanted blood.

The two creatures smashed through the door behind me into the passage and I leapt for the open doorway beyond the old wooden staircase. The girl closed and locked it after me in a flurry of hand movements that seemed to melt into one action.

'This way,' she said and we took off down the back entry. I'm not saying she skated over the cobbles but she moved faster than the things behind us and somehow I was able to keep up with her. We ran for at least a mile and a half. 'In here,' she panted, pressing her weight against a solid-looking door at the back of what looked like an abandoned cinema. The door gave and I squeezed through after her.

'My name's Stella. You're safe now,' she said when she'd got her breath back. I was still bent double. 'You know, if you're going to stick around you'll have to do something about your appearance.'

Stella moved away from me and I saw where we were. Not a cinema at all, but an ice rink. One or two bare bulbs burned, causing the expanse of ice to glow dully beyond the rows of seats. The girl slipped onto the ice. I couldn't imagine how she'd had time to lace up her skating boots.

Chapter Ten

I SENSED THERE was something wrong with my father even before I was told. As I sat on the stairs and watched him carefully thread the buckle of his trench coat and place his trilby on his head, tipping it slightly to one side in the hall mirror, I was aware of feeling vaguely anxious. Maybe it was the way he avoided his own eyes in the glass and just observed the angle of his hat. He would go through into the kitchen to say a quiet goodbye to my mother. I rarely heard what they said to each other at these times. Their voices were a low murmur. Then he would come back into the hall and shout up the stairs, 'Ta-ra, Carl. Look after your mother.' He didn't know I'd been sitting watching him get ready so I would always creep away from the banisters before shouting back, 'Bye'.

He'd open the front door and close it gently behind him and I would run to my room to watch him walk up the street. Always the same, he walked with a relaxed, confident step, nodding at the Hansons in the garden outside their prefab and turning to look behind before crossing the road. I always thought he might see me at that point, but his eyes remained on the road.

I sat in my room for a bit, picking up books and reading the first lines before putting them back, fingering my jam jar filled with half-completed fishing floats made out of pampas grass stems, which Jim, the window cleaner, pinched for me from the garden of the big house at the bottom of Heath Street. I couldn't settle to anything. I turned my little clock radio on but it was always playing 'If You Leave Me Now' by Chicago, so I got up and mooched around the landing and stairs for a couple of minutes, then went downstairs and into the kitchen.

My mother was leaning over the work surface rolling out pastry. There was flour all over the lino around her feet. I looked at the pastry. She'd rolled it completely flat and it had split in a dozen places yet she carried on rolling like a faulty machine and the flour spotted the sleeves of her cardigan and caught in the long dark hair drawn across her face.

How old was I then? Twelve, thirteen? I reached across and took the rolling pin from her. She didn't resist, just pressed her hands against the worktop for support and cried. I hugged her around the waist and felt her body shake. Eventually she turned enough to take me into her arms and we stayed that way for up to a minute. The edge of the worktop was pressing uncomfortably into my back, but, as my father had said, I had to look after my mother. Then I felt foolish because I realised I probably wasn't helping much at all by allowing *her* to comfort *me*.

My mother pulled away and took a paper tissue from her cardigan sleeve. She dabbed at the corners of her eyes and blew her nose. There were little shiny paths running through the powder down her cheeks.

'It's Dad, isn't it?' I said and she started crying again.

I'd seen my mother cry at films on the television but never like this. There had to be something terribly wrong with my father. I knew it couldn't be money or work, or his parents dying, because they were both dead. It had to be his health. He was sick. But how sick?

'What's wrong with him?' I asked, my voice muffled by my mother's leaf-patterned skirt, but she wouldn't tell me.

'He'll be all right,' she said. 'Don't worry. He'll be all right again soon.'

'What is it?' I persisted, crying as well now because I was panicking.

'You don't need to know.'

I did. I did need to know. Not knowing, I felt helpless. Of course, my mother knew I would feel just as helpless if I did know, which was why she didn't tell me.

Over the next few weeks my mind worried at this mystery like a dog working at an old knot of rags. What was wrong with my father? I watched him closely for clues but he was just the same as always with me. Whatever it was that was wrong with him grew like all secrets grow in the minds of children until it assumed terrible proportions. If it was something that couldn't be spoken about then it had to be something to do with some part of him that was taboo even under normal circumstances.

We went out for a day to some woodland about an hour's drive from home. My father drove in his usual calm but firm way. My mother sat wreathed in a cloud of the perfume he always gave her at Christmas. I sat in the back playing with his hat, reading the maker's label – Dunn & Co – and stroking the feather in the chequered band. After walking in the woods for a mile or two – sometimes I ran on ahead kicking through the leaves and could hear them talking in low voices behind me – we stopped for lunch at a pine-panelled cafeteria. My father said I could have ten pence if I would eat a piece of Blue Stilton. I put it in my mouth and tried to swallow without chewing it. He gave me the ten pence but I couldn't swallow the cheese and I had to spit it out. He and my mother laughed along with the people on the next table and he took back his ten pence.

All the time we were out I was worrying about him and guessing what might be wrong with him. I decided that for it to be such an unspeakable problem it had to have something to do with going to the toilet, so when my father announced after the cheese and biscuits that he was going to the toilet I got up and said I was going as well. I waited for a look to pass between him and my mother but there was none. I followed him nervously to the door marked GENTLEMEN. If this was going to be the moment of truth he might take the opportunity to talk to me about it. Suddenly I didn't want to know and I almost turned back but he'd reached the door and was holding it open for me. I smelt the disinfectant and dirty hand-towels and had to go in.

My father and I stood at neighbouring stalls – the first time I could remember us doing that – and I looked, because I had to.

It was all there and I couldn't see anything wrong. When we left the gents I was doubly relieved.

If not that though, I started thinking as we got back to the table, what *was* wrong with him?

I found out a couple of weeks later. I crept downstairs one Wednesday night and listened outside the lounge door as my mother and father talked. They still had the television on and the door was closed, so it was not easy to follow their conversation. But I did manage to hear the odd word and half-sentence. When I heard the word 'Christie's' I experienced a sudden, awful sinking feeling in my stomach and a chill spread from there to grip my entire body. I tiptoed upstairs so the sound of crying wouldn't alert them to my presence.

Christie's was the cancer hospital where several of my mother's relatives had died. My father's aunt, also, had spent her last two weeks there. I'd never been, but the name of the place terrified me. It was synonymous with cancer, which in those days and in my experience meant suffering and death.

It had been at the back of my mind, buried deep beneath layers of denial and fear, ever since I'd known my father was ill. Even to utter the hospital's name was to tempt fate and hasten the inevitable.

I spoke to my mother the following morning while my father was out of the house.

'Dad's got cancer, hasn't he?' I said. I was hurting too much to realise how insensitive I was being to my mother's feelings. She looked at me for a moment, tears brimming at her eyes, but I felt angry. I wanted to be treated like an adult.

'He has, hasn't he?' I persisted.

'No, Carl, he hasn't,' my mother said, kneeling down and holding my arms.

'He has leukaemia. It's like cancer but it's different.' She was trying to make it seem better than it was by giving it a name which wasn't cancer – a word which in our house was usually lip-read – but because of the Christie's connection I knew exactly what kind of illness my father had.

'Is he going to die?' I asked, my voice on the edge of breaking.

'I hope not, love. I hope he'll be all right. If you hope so too, as hard as you can, it might help him.'

I started to cry. Standing there in front of my mother I just gave in and the tears tumbled from my eyes. She gathered me into a fierce hug. I couldn't stop once I'd started. My eyes hurt, I was short of breath, my head ached and still the tears fell, soaking my mother's shoulder. She stroked my hair and said, 'What, love, what?' when I tried to speak.

'I'm sorry,' I said. 'I'm sorry. I'm sorry.'

'Ssh, ssh. Stop crying. Try and be strong for your father. It'll help him.'

By the time he came back inside I was in my room pretending to be engrossed in making floats and my mother was polishing the brasses in the lounge.

I didn't tell my father I knew but I gathered that my mother had told him. We never spoke about the disease or the hospital and I did my best to be strong. At night after I'd gone to bed I'd slide out and kneel on the floor and pray for him, whispering the words so they wouldn't be heard downstairs but would be loud enough for God to hear if He was listening. I didn't believe in God but if my father died and I'd left a stone unturned I knew I'd never forgive myself.

A few days later my mother told me my father had been receiving treatment for months. When I thought he'd been doing shift work he was actually walking to Navigation Road, getting a train to Stretford, then a 22 bus to Christie's. He didn't take the car because the treatment left him feeling too groggy to drive home afterwards. And he refused the ambulance they offered to take him home in so that I wouldn't look out of my bedroom window and get the shock of my life.

* * *

WHEN I WOKE up in the abandoned ice rink, slumped on a wooden bench, Stella had come off the ice and was wearing a big old blue sweater. She'd exchanged her skates for a pair of heavy boots, and a pair of thick woolly tights. She made me a cup of what passed for coffee in the City. It tasted like dust and was pitch-black – 'There's no milk' – but it was hot and wet.

'What are you doing here?' I asked her when we'd been talking for a while.

'Most people can't remember how they got here,' she said. 'They've just blanked out on it. But I still can. The details have gone but I can still just about remember the big picture.' She sipped her own coffee. 'I was a skater. It was all I lived for. I was no good at anything else and I dreamed of skating for England. They wrote about me in the local paper. I was prodigiously talented, they said. But I went too far. I did a quintuple salchow one day at the local rink. It's not supposed to be possible. It means you spin five times in the air. It's just not possible. But I did it. I got enough height and I was light enough. Somehow I did it. I knew I'd done it. I felt sick when I landed.

'Only one person had seen me. I saw this woman staring at me like she'd seen a ghost. Her mouth hanging open, her eyes all wide. She's here now as well. I've seen her a couple of times but she doesn't remember a thing. I tried to talk to her but she was suspicious so I've steered clear ever since.'

'How did it happen?' I asked. 'How did you end up here?'

'On the way home from the ice rink I was grabbed by someone hiding in bushes next to the railway line. I can't remember anything after that.'

'Haven't you tried to get back?'

'It's impossible. There's no way back.'

'There must be,' I insisted.

'People have gone mad trying. It doesn't matter how far they walk, there's no escape route. It's hard enough to get out of the City and even if you manage that you're faced with miles and miles of the Waste. People have wandered there for up to a year and stumbled back into the City completely mad. The contours change and you lose all sense of orientation. Only two people have made it beyond the Waste and into the Dark.'

'What the fuck is the Dark?' I asked.

'The Dark defies all the laws of nature. It's always dark, as if it were night-time, only day and night don't have any meaning there. At least we've got light and dark in the City. There are no dimensions to the Dark. It just goes on and on in all directions, like space. If you do go into the Dark your only hope is the one in a million chance that you accidentally wander back into the Waste. There's no way out the other side because there is no other side.'

'Who are the two people you mentioned who've been into the Dark? Did they come back? I want to meet them.'

'You can't. One man's in an institution. Hasn't spoken a word of sense in five years. The other one escaped and is roaming the City somewhere.'

'Why didn't I come through the Dark on my way into the City?'

'It's a one-way thing. It's only there going out.'

'How do you know all this?' I asked, pulling my squashed pack of Camels from out of my boot and lighting one. They were almost all gone.

'I'm an outlaw. I'm outside society. I don't take the drugs, don't read the propaganda. I'm not on record. Some people slip in through the net. Like you did.'

'Only now they're after me.' I took a deep drag and felt my head swim.

'They've been after me for years. You just have to remain one step ahead. You have to think like them. The point is, they're only really after one person – whoever it was who killed the bloody king – but no one is above suspicion. You're assumed to be guilty here until proven innocent. And nobody's going to expend energy on your behalf trying to prove you innocent. Everyone remains guilty of harbouring the assassin until he is caught and justice is done.'

'I can guess what form that might take,' I said.

'If money meant anything here, there'd be a bounty on his head,' she said. 'As it is, there's an enthusiastic vigilante movement. Everyone's eager to prove they're not guilty. That's why you have to do something about your appearance. You won't last long looking like that.'

I took a long drag on my cigarette and thought about how long I'd been growing my hair, how much I loved my white leather jacket and my butterfly boots.

'I know someone,' she said.

Ten minutes later we were peeling away the corrugated iron sheeting that blocked the inside of the door to discourage intruders. Stella had smeared dust and grime on my jacket to make us less conspicuous. It would take about half an hour to go across town to Eyshall, the district where Stella's friend Maxi lived. Maxi was an actress and she kept a well-stocked wardrobe. In the meantime Stella had given

me a black woollen beanie like Giff's and I tucked the
rest of my hair down the back of my jacket, but there
was nothing we could do about my boots. Stella's
feet were several sizes smaller than mine.

It was dark outside. I had no idea of the time.
My watch had stopped when I'd entered the City.
I asked Stella but she just shrugged and said, 'Keep
close to me.' We walked in the shadow of buildings,
turning our heads away whenever we passed anyone.
At first the streets were fairly quiet but it clearly
wasn't curfew hour yet and the nearer we came
to the city centre the more people we saw. At one
intersection we passed right beneath a judge's nose,
Stella claiming that was less obvious than crossing
the road to avoid him.

'Turn down here,' Stella said, taking us into a
quieter district of bigger, grander-looking terraced
houses with imposing gateposts and steps up to the
front doors. The windows were all black as night
and there was no noise coming from within. A few
of the windows on the top floors betrayed shadows
flitting across pulled blinds but Stella hurried on
and I didn't have time to linger. I heard a ringing
telephone but again Stella led me on deeper into the
City. We turned back towards the light and the noise
after two more blocks and soon found ourselves in
a crowd of murmuring bystanders lining the sides
of a main road. Stella motioned to me to keep my
head down. I tried to listen to the voices around me
but there was only an indistinguishable mutter, like
extras mumbling lines of nonsense in a film.

'What's going on?' I whispered to Stella.

She shook her head. 'They're obviously waiting
for something,' she said. 'I think we ought to wait
quietly or we'll draw attention to ourselves.'

I nodded and reached into my boot for my squashed pack of Camels. Stella saw me and pushed my hand back down. From the breast pocket of her jacket she produced a drab soft pack which she passed to me. I examined the pack. There was no brand name, just the word CIGARETTES and a logo that was a rough spiral design. I shrugged and tipped one out of the packet. Stella struck a match for me and I took a drag of what tasted like the paper straws we used to light on the Bunsen burners in school physics lessons. I scowled and Stella smiled grimly.

'I know,' she said. 'Tastes like shit but there's not a lot of choice here.' Then she looked up because there was movement in the crowd. Heads were turning towards the road and necks craning. I heard an engine approaching; it sounded like a big truck. It rumbled closer and I could see from the cab that it was a very old worn-out haulage vehicle. Proceeding at walking pace it was escorted by paramilitaries wearing black drill and brandishing wooden clubs. They wore black woollen hats similar to the one Stella had given me to wear. She noticed me fingering it and I left it alone. The paramilitaries looked into the crowd with eyes that were chips of black ice. Occasionally one of them would heft his club.

The vehicle was pulling a trailer like an open cattle truck in which were packed at least thirty prisoners, staring wide-eyed and sallow-faced at the crowds as they were drawn past. Their heads had been shaved roughly, nicking the scalp here and there and leaving short trails of dried blood. A few tufts of hair remained behind the ears or at the temple. I thought of the Passage.

The reaction of the crowd was curious. They watched the approach of the trailer, then bowed their heads as the prisoners passed right by them as if to avoid the vacant stares, and once it had moved on they looked up again, catching the steady but blank gazes of the few creatures standing at the back of the trailer. Then one or two hollow cries went up – 'Traitors', 'Murderers', 'King killers' – and the crowd started to disperse.

'Where are they being taken?' I asked Stella after we'd crossed the road and plunged down another side street.

'To die,' she said. 'But first they get driven all around the City to set an example.'

'*Set an example*?' I said sharply.

'Yes, why?' she said.

'Nothing,' I said. 'A line in a song.' The lyrics to 'Shave Your Head' hovered just out of reach. Something about setting an example, starting a trend.

For some reason I thought of Annie Risk and I felt a little kick in my stomach. I didn't know how long I'd been in the City but it must have been at least a couple of days and she was bound to have tried to call me. Unable to get me at home she would have tried the shop and there would have been no answer there either. She would be worried and there was nothing I could do. For the time being I had to go along with Stella's advice in order to give myself a chance merely of surviving in the City. Stella had said there was no way out but given that I'd found the place – I'd begun to suspect partly because I'd been so convinced it did actually exist – I had to believe there was a route out of it. My belief would help me find one. Perhaps the day I gave up believing it was possible would be the day I became a true citizen of the benighted place.

'What?' said Stella, looking at me.

'Nothing.'

We entered a large square. A cluster of taxi cabs dozed by a small section of railing, their engines switched off and lumpy figures slumped over in the driving seats. An articulated bus bent almost double waited for daylight to come. A few bits of newsprint, damp old cigarette packets bearing the same spiral design as Stella's and plastic drinks bottles whispered under our feet as we crossed the wide road and headed for a narrow bridge.

'It must be near curfew,' I said.

'We'll just make it,' Stella answered without looking back. 'We're in Eyshall now.'

I didn't know how she was able to be so accurate without a watch but I didn't question her. As we walked across the little bridge I looked over the parapet and at first it was too dark to see anything. I heard Stella's shoes on the road and knew I should catch up with her but I wanted to know all there was to know about my surroundings. As I concentrated and shielded my eyes from the bleak street lighting either side of the bridge I could make out the black, treacly canal beneath. It moved slowly, bearing a patina of litter and patches of scum. The banks were reinforced with stone slabs. It was narrow and there was very little room beneath the bridge, yet despite its unwelcoming aspect I felt reassured by the mere presence of another element in this restrictive landscape.

I heard Stella's voice hissing in the distance. Looking up the road I saw her a good fifty yards away beckoning me from beneath a broken street lamp.

Chapter Eleven

MAXI'S PLACE WAS an old dentist's surgery. She had the reclining chair, the pull-down light, wall-mounted cabinets with mirrored fronts, little instrument trolleys from which she served drinks. She even still had the drill, one of the old, slow motor-driven kind with long extendible arms and strings. I shuddered in recollection.

'What would you like, Carl?' Maxi asked. 'To drink?'

I had a small glass of the City's fruit brandy. Although clearly made from tinned fruit, it was less vile than the cigarettes. Since we were inside and Stella had indicated Maxi's place was quite safe, I took out my Camels and offered the pack around. Both women smoked but preferred their own brand. I lit up and at Maxi's invitation sat down in the reclining chair.

Maxi was a tiny woman, more like a little girl dressed up in her mother's clothes, and she wore exaggerated make-up which made her look slightly clownish. I assumed she changed before going out, like Stella swopping her skating tutu for a baggy jumper and leggings.

'How come you've got this place?' I asked Maxi.

She looked at Stella who replied for her. 'Dental care is not a priority in the City. Most people don't live long enough to lose their teeth. We perform our own extractions if necessary.'

I winced.

'There are lots of squats like this,' Stella said. 'We might be able to find you something similar.'

'I'm not planning to stick around long enough to put down roots, but thanks for the offer.'

Maxi spoke to me. 'Stella says you need a new look.'

I shrugged. 'What do you think?'

'I'm surprised you're still walking around.' She jumped to her feet. 'So let's get started.'

I sat back in the chair and Maxi came up behind me, taking a handful of my hair. I wanted to wriggle out of her grasp and run away. I was attached to my hair. But before I realised what she was doing she was sawing through it with a huge pair of dressmaker's scissors. In dismay I watched my magnificent mane hit the floor. Let go, I told myself. It'll grow back.

Maxi continued cutting. My impression was that she was more enthusiastic than proficient. Her scissors tugged at my scalp. It seemed to me she wasn't taking a lot of care to layer the cut and I would more than likely have to pay a visit to Jerry's Gentlemen's Barbers when I got back to London. I suddenly felt overwhelmingly homesick. When I'd started to let my hair grow I still went back to see Jerry and watch him do his stuff on a couple of customers. It only ever took him the time it took to smoke one cigarette. He'd stick a Raffles between his lips, light up and start working his magic scissors. He never took the cigarette out of his mouth but instead let the ash droop until inevitably it fell into your hair and he dealt with it in his next stroke.

'That's enough, surely,' I said sharply, coming back to my senses as Maxi yanked too hard again.

'Not really,' said Stella, who must have been watching from behind.

'Let me see,' I insisted. 'Give me a mirror.'

Stella handed Maxi a mirror and she held it behind my head. I sat up to see myself reflected in one of the cabinet doors and there was only a split second in it: I saw Maxi's eyes sliding away from a door in the far corner of the room and knew I'd been set up. For some reason I felt Stella wasn't part of it so I shouted, 'Stella, get out of here *now*,' as I launched myself from the chair, batting a hand backwards to ward off Maxi's scissors just in case. Even as I was still turning, the door in the far corner burst inward and a spitting, frenzied ball of vicious flesh and teeth spun into the room.

Stella had gone for the door we'd come in by but already my way was cut off by the intruders. I whirled around as they came for me. There were windows – my only hope. In one fluid movement I yanked the overhead light from above the chair and had enough leverage on it to smash it into the nearest attacker's face. Maxi clutched the scissors to her chest, clearly hoping her stillness and twisted loyalty would stand her in good stead with them. I didn't much care. OK, she'd double-crossed me and Stella, but that was nothing compared to what she'd done to my hair. I plucked the scissors from her hand and as the second creature leapt I thrust them out in front of me. It gored itself spectacularly, spraying Maxi and me with steaming hot blood.

They were like the things that had come for me in the record shop.

The other one was already regaining its stance and I sensed more creatures or shock troops about to emerge from the far door, so I picked up the instrument trolley, bottles of fruit brandy toppling and smashing on the tiled surgery floor, and hurled it at the biggest window. I followed it, shielding my face with my arm, and fell into the street in a roll. I picked myself up and ran. I knew that more of them would be after me within seconds.

I ran over the little bridge over the canal, thought about jumping down onto the tow path but before I'd had chance to consider it I was halfway across the big square. I could hear faint cries behind me. I hoped Stella was safe. There was no sign of her and no evidence of anyone else. Just to add to my problems it was obviously curfew now as well. The thought of forcing open the concertina doors and hiding in the articulated bus occurred to me as well but as an idea it was only marginally better than shinning up a street lamp and hoping to stay up there until my pursuers got bored and slunk away, tails, if they had them, between their legs. Creatures like these didn't get bored. They were perfect machines.

I turned off as soon as there was a side street to turn into, then immediately took a left and then a right, until I had lost all sense of direction. Some bizarre logic suggested that if I lost my way the things would lose theirs too, as if they were somehow in my control. I ran through nameless streets that all looked the same. My heart was pumping furiously, my head amazingly clear. I was sorry to have lost Stella and felt soiled after almost becoming trapped in Maxi's sticky web of betrayal. At least I'd managed to make a mess of her post-modern surgery squat, I thought with grim satisfaction, but then realised I didn't actually hold a grudge against her. In this city you had to sell yourself and others in order to postpone your ride in the open-topped trailer I'd seen earlier that evening.

I stopped for breath. The night was humid and prickly. Bent over, hands on knees, I listened but couldn't hear the creatures any more. Could I really have outrun them?

No clatter of pursuit, but the telephone was loud and clear in the night.

It was only a couple of streets away, or so it seemed. I had to stop it ringing before it attracted unwelcome attention. As I ran I caught sight of my reflection in the oily blackness of a ground-floor window. My hair was uneven and scraggy. If anything I stuck out more than before. From my pocket I pulled out the black beanie Stella had given me and put it on.

I stopped in front of the house the ringing was coming from. The air was very still and heavy like just before a storm, the streets behind me quiet, but I sensed my pursuers couldn't be far away. I ran up the three steps, stepped across to the window ledge and smashed a single pane with my elbow. Reaching in to release the catch, I jumped down into the room, landing as softly as an eleven-stone man in cowboy boots can.

I followed the ringing out of the front room and into the hall which was cast in a ghostly half-light by coloured glass in the front door. The end of the hall, however, lay in darkness. I walked slowly, my heart hammering, sweat trickling down the back of my neck. There were two doors. I opened the first and stepped inside.

I looked across to the far side of the room. There was something there but it wasn't a telephone. I stood there for a few seconds feeling every hair on my body stand stiffly erect. Fear filled me up like gas fills up a room.

I took three steps back, turned around and closed the door behind me. I twisted the knob to open the second door and suddenly the ringing was much louder. I could see the telephone sitting like a lobster on a table covered with a sheet. Feeble starlight made the room's shadows grainy and thick. There seemed to be dust sheets covering all the furniture and the sheets were smeared with something dark. The deep carpet impeded my progress, catching at my boot heels.

I picked up the receiver and the sudden silence seemed louder than the persistent ringing. The Bakelite felt clammy in my hand and the receiver slipped as I lifted it to my ear. A woman's hysterical voice screamed down the line – 'Carl! Help! Come quickly, Carl! Please!' – then was cut off.

I stood there in the darkness, cold and alone, as the line buzzed.

I knew the voice on the line. It was Annie Risk's.

I RATTLED THE cradle but the connection had been severed. I dialled Annie's number and listened to the rustle of digits down the line. To my amazement the ringing tone sprang up at the other end and then stopped as the phone was picked up. My heart in my mouth, I waited for a voice.

'Hello?'

It was Annie's voice.

'Annie,' I said. 'It's Carl.'

'Hello? Who is it? Hello?' She sounded anxious.

'Annie, it's me. Was that you before ringing here? Annie, what's wrong?

'Who is this?' Panic caused her voice to break. She couldn't hear me. I could hear her but she couldn't hear me. To her it was just a wrong number. She'd be hearing those odd metallic scratchy sounds I'd heard both at the flat and at the shop when I'd picked up the phone and there'd been no one there. Then, out of the terrible silence, came her voice again, barely a whisper: '*Carl?*'

I shivered.

'Annie, it's me,' I shouted.

Silence.

'Carl. Is that you? Are you there? Carl!' She broke down and cried. 'Carl. Oh Carl.'

I shouted her name again but she obviously couldn't hear me. For a few moments all I could hear down the line was the sound of her quietly crying. Then the line went dead and a tremor passed through me.

Some time later I came to, roused by thunder outside. I was sitting in one of the armchairs. I felt a terrible emptiness, like you feel when you wake up and realise it wasn't a dream and your life really is spinning out of control. Rain beat against the windows like the feet of small animals. The dust-sheet beneath my hands was damp and sticky. I pushed myself to my feet. I had to get on. As I reached a standing position and stretched my body backwards a flash of lightning outside turned the room momentarily to daylight and imprinted its shocking colours on my retinas.

The sheets, which I had thought merely grimy with age, were stained with blood, and from its vivid shade I knew it was not long spilt. A thunderclap shook the room, rattling the windows in their frames. My flesh crawled as I strained to see into the corners but, dark again, they guarded their secrets. I backed away to the door and just as my hand closed on the knob another jagged flash of pure white light lit up the room. There was red everywhere. Even the carpet was tufted and matted with blood. I turned and fled.

In the dark hall another lightning flash burst in through the half-light at the far end. As if someone were taking pictures of me. There was nowhere to turn. I knew I had to go back into the first room and confront what lay there. I opened the door. A thundercrack made my breastbone vibrate. I walked across the dark, tacky floor towards the figure in the bed.

There was a drip stand at the head of the bed and tubes threaded into the patient's pale arm.

'Oh God,' I whispered.

Lightning stripped the bed bare of shadows and I saw the bruised, bloodshot eyes staring right at me. They were not my father's eyes, but mine.

Part Three

'This king, *his* king, remained such a stranger and so inaccessible that he was no more than an abstraction, no longer even a symbol, and in no way a human being; Boris came quite naturally to doubt the reality of his existence.'

Alain Robbe-Grillet, *Un Régicide*

Chapter Twelve

MY FATHER'S LIFE seemed to diminish in every respect. When he was in the house he would be sitting talking in the lounge with my mother. The door would be closed and the radio playing quietly to cover their voices. I sat on the stairs and listened a couple of times. He never turned the radio up quite loud enough, so I could hear most of what they said to each other. It was practical stuff. The doctors had given him between three and eighteen months. I heard him telling my mother with an even voice how he was going to make sure there was enough money for us both. Most of the time she wouldn't say anything and when she did I could hear the strain in her voice. She was fighting to keep her emotions under control. Sometimes she couldn't and I heard her voice break, I heard her sobbing, and pictured my father putting his arm around her and the two of them sitting there on the settee staring at the gas fire.

I sat shivering on the stairs, part of me wishing I could sit with them and part of me too frightened to behold their faces while they talked about death. Also, I knew that my presence would make it harder for both of them.

When he was home but not well enough to sit with my mother, he would be up in his bedroom, which was now a sickroom. I didn't go near it, if I could help it. Once I heard him calling me and at first I tried to ignore it. I looked out of my window at my mother kneeling down in the soil and tearing away at the bindweed that was choking her garden. Whenever she thought she'd destroyed a section it always grew back stronger than before, and it spread so quickly she was unable to keep up with it. But, being my mother, she didn't give up. It wasn't in her nature.

My father was still calling me. I went and stood outside his bedroom door, thinking that if he didn't call again I'd leave him.

'Carl.' I could hear the effort he was putting into trying to make his voice sound normal.

I turned the doorknob and went in. The curtains were drawn across the windows even though it was mid-morning. Drawn curtains with daylight filtering through them have always depressed me since then.

'It hurts my eyes,' he said, lying on his side facing the empty half of the bed, his head completely bald.

The room smelt stuffy and damp. The illness was causing him to sweat a lot; my mother changed the sheets every day. I stood awkwardly, shifting my weight from one leg to the other, wondering what he wanted to say.

'You mustn't worry, Carl,' he said eventually. 'Neither you nor your mother must worry about anything. I'll be up and about soon.'

His words rang hollow but in fact he was right. By the end of the week he was dressed and feeling much better. He looked like his old self. My mother's face was gaunt and tense, as if she were expecting him to relapse at any moment. I was more naive, hoping the illness was in remission.

He started taking me to new places. I was still on my summer holidays so we had plenty of time. Sometimes my mother came with us and tried to enjoy herself, but with her it was as if I could see through the costumes and make-up and around the back of the set. The big man she'd loved all her life was dying. She knew and I knew it, even if he smiled and tilted his hat, and it was too painful for her. One day when my father was out – getting treatment – I caught her looking through old photograph albums. The fading brownish snaps of the two of them honeymooning on the north-west coast. The family groups in which the baby was me, but I was still too young to be able to see myself like that. My mother and father's life before I was born and while I was tiny had always been a series of still images as far as I was concerned, but now I realised they'd had a life together and they were looking at the end of it coming up to meet them before they were half done with it.

I went into the garden and tugged at a fresh patch of bindweed.

My father took me walking in the Peaks, bog-trotting across the crumbly peat of Black Hill, clambering up the dried-up Kinder Downfall and wandering around lost in the mist on top of Kinder Scout. One Wednesday night he said we were going somewhere special. I asked if Mum was coming with us and he said it wasn't her type of thing. This was at the tea table and my mother was there, smiling and nodding.

'I know *you'll* enjoy it though,' she said to me, passing me the plate of buttered malt loaf.

As I was putting my anorak on and my father was buttoning his trench coat I saw my mother mouth something at my father. He nodded and said, 'I've got it.' I looked at his coat and saw something bulky in the pocket. I had no idea what it was and I didn't ask. My father put his trilby on, tilting it in the hall mirror, and we stepped outside into the still-warm evening.

'Why do we need coats?' I asked.

'It might not stay warm where we're going,' my father said as he led the way to the bus stop. I thought about asking why we were going on the bus instead of in the car, but thought that, like with the bulky thing in my father's coat pocket, it might be better not to ask. I didn't want to spoil the surprise by finding out too early.

It was already quite late in the summer holidays and the sun was setting as we rode towards town on the 263 bus through the suburb where I was born and later past the end of the road where my father was born. I glanced at him and he looked down and smiled at me from under the brim of his hat, then looked back out of the window. I wondered what was going through his mind. His face looked calm. He was probably excited by the thought of where we were going and how much it would mean to me. But he must also have been plagued by thoughts of the underlying reason for making this trip. I had already sensed on our walking excursions in the Peaks that he was trying to cram into a few short months the activities a father and son might normally spread over several years.

I didn't twig where we were going until we got off near Moss Side and walked down narrow terraced streets that soon were resounding to the cobble-slap of Doc Martens and trainers as hundreds and soon thousands of men and boys in football scarves streamed in towards Maine Road. We stopped at a corner and my father reached into his pocket and pulled out a brand-new sky-blue, maroon and white striped scarf. As he tied it gently around my neck and I looked at his coat collar, unable to meet his eyes, I could hear him wheezing. He straightened up, ruffled my hair and we walked on.

I looked down back entries as we passed them. Fans strode out of each one to thread into the main flow. It was a great feeling, to be part of this huge mass of people all going to the same place, carried along on a tide of anticipation. I was glad of the scarf – it made me feel I belonged, just as my father had known it would.

Soon I could hear the roar of the crowd in the stadium and my heart beat fast. There was a lump in my throat that was only partly due to the occasion. We rounded the last corner and there was the ground, rearing up massive and monumental before me. I'd been a fan for years but going to games was never even a consideration because we couldn't afford it. My father bought me a programme and as we reached the top of a flight of steps I suddenly saw this huge shocking expanse of green, vivid under the spotlights. I looked at my father and I saw the same innocent surprise in his eyes as well. I had a thought.

'How many matches have you been to?' I asked him.

'Oh, I don't know,' he began. I could see him weighing up alternatives. 'I mean, when I was a boy…' He rubbed his nose.

I looked back at the pitch and in a small voice he said, 'I haven't been before.'

I gripped his hand for a moment.

'Come on,' he said, turning and leading me away. 'We'll have to get to our seats. Don't want to miss the kick-off.'

The match was almost unbearably exciting. I watched my heroes in action. I was close enough to hear them calling for the ball. It wouldn't have mattered if they'd lost but they won, 3-1. We moved up two positions in the league that night and I took a big step closer to my father.

It was painful but I learnt a lot from both my mother and father in those weeks, about love and how to treat those who are precious to you.

I RAN OUT into the night and the raging storm, careless of dogs and police and vigilante patrols, intent only on putting as much distance as possible between me and that house. The body in the bed. The rooms full of blood. The telephone that may or may not have allowed me to hear Annie Risk's voice on the other end. Even if it was her voice she certainly couldn't hear me. In the confusion I gave in to fear and just ran.

Maybe I was lucky. Perhaps I had a guardian angel or I was blessed with a good sense of direction. Possibly the map was as much inside my head as printed on a scrap of paper. Whatever, however, I found my way back to Stella's abandoned ice rink. I yanked the door open and tore at the corrugated iron.

I was stopped in my tracks by a banshee yell and a ball of fury rushing towards me. Before I knew what was happening there was a long blade quivering under my chin.

'You should be more careful,' Stella said, withdrawing the knife. 'Were you followed?'

'I don't know,' I said, taking a deep breath. I don't think so. I didn't see anyone.'

She reached behind me to close the door and drag the corrugated iron sheet across.

'You must need a drink,' she said, leading the way to her living quarters.

'When did you get back?' I asked. It suddenly occurred to me that for all I knew she might have been in on the betrayal.

'Maxi must have been put under pressure,' she said, second-guessing me again. 'Friends do shop each other but only when they need to in order to survive. It's not safe to stay here much longer. Hence the welcome I gave you just then.'

I didn't tell Stella about breaking into the house to answer the telephone, nor about what I'd seen in the first room. After all, I still didn't know what she'd been doing upstairs at the second-hand record shop. I told her I'd made my way back slowly through the storm, picking my way carefully so as to avoid pursuit. I did, however, ask if there was a telephone in the ice rink. She said no: there were very few at all in the City and, as far as she was aware, they were good only for local calls and all lines were monitored. I could believe that.

I stayed with Stella long enough to dry my clothes out and get warm again. She offered to tidy up my hair. 'You can see how nervous Maxi was,' she said, running a pair of nail scissors over the worst bits. 'Normally she's an excellent stylist.' But I was restless. Having heard Annie Risk's voice, clearly in distress, I knew I had to try anything to get out of the City. I asked Stella about the men she had mentioned who had been into the Dark and stumbled back into the City.

Both were beyond reach, she said, committed to institutions for the criminally insane.

'I must be able to get to them,' I said.

'Impossible. You'd be killed before you got close.'

'Which of the two is the more accessible?' I pressed.

'A man called Gledhill,' she said with a sigh. 'They keep him in King's Hospital. That's all I know.'

She told me the way to King's and said, 'You can't go now, Carl. You need sleep and it's still curfew.'

'Stella,' I said, 'thanks for all you've done, but I've got to go.'

She protested but held the corrugated iron guard aside for me as I climbed out. The rain had stopped, leaving pavements glistening under the orange lights. I walked quickly, running with as light and swift a step as possible across roads, and peering down back entries, alert to every sound and movement. The tail end of the storm blew around the rooftops, shaking trees and curtain rags behind broken windows. I found myself humming the keyboard riff from 'Fear' by the Passage and I pictured Annie Risk, her body illuminated by orange street light. The riff matched my quick, stealthy march. I'd only been to Annie's flat twice, had only known her a few weeks but as the only link between this world and hers – that frightened voice on the phone line – she was assuming almost iconic significance. I'd even begun seeing her in Stella, which had been another reason for wanting to leave the ice rink without delay.

I stopped dead in my tracks. A splash of white light on the wall diagonally opposite could only come from a car headlamp. I crouched in a doorway and waited. The car turned into the street where I was hiding. I didn't know if it was police or the dubious Giff and his associates. Either way I preferred my own company. The car crawled closer and I curled into a ball. Peeping out I saw the driver – wearing a black boiler suit bristling with badges – switch on a spotlight and angle it manually at the doorways on the other side of the street. He swept the beam back and forth while his colleague in the passenger seat had a good look. In a moment he'd swap to my side of the street and that would be my short cut to the even closer haircut and the open-topped bus.

The car crept forward. He switched the light across.

A matter of inches.

Had the car been travelling two miles an hour more slowly the beam would have caught me. Instead it hit the brickwork six inches to my right. Consequently I was plunged into deeper shadow and they never saw me. But they could almost have heard the thump of my heart or my sigh of relief. Only when the car had turned right at the end of the street did I uncurl my long body, stretch painfully and dart to the junction. I looked right and saw the police car turning right again. I went left and ran like a bastard.

I didn't know how I was going to get into the hospital. Maybe I was relying on there being some wall to climb, a window to lever open.

King's Hospital was a fortress. Floodlights bathed the front entrance on the main road, so I trotted down the smaller road at the side. There was a wall all right, but it was twice my height and offered few footholds. I ran on, asking myself if this was a stupid idea. I reached the end of the wall. It turned left and seemed to extend without a break into the night. I ran along it at a crouch. There were no openings. Then I noticed a section of railing on the other side of the street and went across to take a look. It was a canal. I leap-frogged the railing and scrambled down a muddy slope to the tow-path. There was just enough width and height to make it under the road. I bent down and crawled into the tunnel. It was dark and stank of sewage but if I was lucky it might just yield a stage door entrance to the hospital.

After twenty-five yards the ceiling lifted and I was able to proceed at full height. There was a soft phosphorescent glow hovering over the water, by which I could make out where to place my feet without tripping. A large opening came into view on my side. I guessed it was a waste outlet coming from the hospital. Looking ahead, there were no more breaks in the wall as far as I could see, which admittedly wasn't very far but I was in a hurry. So I ducked into the waste pipe. The stench was nauseating but I held my insides together by force of will and splashed through the trickle of canal-bound effluent, humming 'Watching You Dance'. I held my breath as the pipe became steeper for a few yards and then levelled out and the ceiling disappeared. I peered over the side. This section of the pipe ran through a yard at the back of the hospital, uncovered perhaps to allow extra waste to be tipped in by hand.

I clambered up into the yard and walked over to a rickety-looking door. It opened at my touch and I stiffened. Far off I could hear a buzz of talk and the clang of instruments or cutlery in a sink. I walked away from these sounds to the first intersection of passageways and looked down a long, unpainted corridor lit by a string of bare off-white bulbs. I crept down the corridor, glancing in at every window in every door I passed. I saw rooms full of lockers and dissection tables, rows of lecture-room desks and chairs, pigeon-holes stuffed with files and notes. No sign of any staff and no noise, save the odd dripping tap.

I reached a turning signposted Haematology and Secure Unit. I turned down the new corridor and when another junction pointed left to the Secure Unit I went that way.

Maybe I'd gained access the back way and comers from other directions would face tighter security, or the Secure Unit was not quite as described. I walked straight into a long, drab ward with beds down both sides, most unoccupied, a few curtained off and billowing with shadows. Something told me to keep going through the ward and into a second, L-shaped room. The walls were whitewashed, temperature and lighting kept low. I walked silently towards the corner and hugged the wall, waiting for my breathing to steady, listening for any sound coming from around the corner.

All was quiet.

Slowly I slid along the wall and angled my head to see around the corner.

There was a bed, a hard-looking chair and a tall man.

The man was standing up looking out of the window, his back to me. I stepped into his territory, my boot heel clicking on the wooden floor.

'Who are you?' the man asked without looking around. I focused on his reflection and realised he had been watching me in the window. Disarmed, I came to a halt.

'My name is Carl,' I said. 'You don't know me. Are you Gledhill?' My heart was hammering. Although my gut feeling about the man was good, it was still possible he was one of theirs. Or, if he was insane as it was claimed, he could be dangerous. Alternatively, if he felt threatened he probably only had to call and help would come running.

'What do you want, Carl?' He turned from the window and looked at me with sad, dark eyes. I moved forward two steps and he went to lie down on the bed, offering me the chair with a casual gesture. I lowered myself onto the chair without taking my eyes off him. His face had once been handsome but the left side was now somewhat twisted out of true and his mouth didn't close properly.

'It's not safe for you here, you know,' he said, looking away from me and fixing his gaze on the ceiling. 'They come and see me at irregular intervals. I haven't had a visit for six hours at least. You haven't got long.'

I sensed a terrible sadness, an emptiness that was the antithesis of my urgent need to flee the City. He had the aura of a man who had tried everything and failed. Being in his company depressed me.

'What are you doing here?' I asked him, keeping my senses alert to the approach of hospital staff.

'I went too far,' he said in a flat voice.

'You mean the Dark?' I asked in a whisper.

He winced and turned onto his side. He was a lean man, his skin displaying an unhealthy mustardy pallor. If he was more prisoner than patient, however, why was he left unguarded in an unlocked room?

I got up and walked around to the other side of the bed so I could see his face. 'How did you come to the City?' I asked him.

'I went too far,' he repeated, his lips barely moving. 'Too fast.'

'What do you mean?'

'I did what they said couldn't be done.'

My stomach tightened. 'What?'

'I ran a mile in three and a half minutes. I collapsed at the tape and woke up here.'

'You mean the City?'

He suddenly shot out a hand and gripped my arm. His grip was pitiful.

'Go now,' he ordered.

'I have to know about the Dark,' I said, leaning closer to him.

'Stay away.'

What did he mean? From him or the Dark? 'I have to get out of the City. Getting into the Dark seems to be the only way. I need to know where it is. How do I get there?'

'It's all around us.'

A ring around the City like Stella had said? 'I just walk outwards from the City in any direction?'

He tightened his grip on my arm and drew me right up to his face. His eyes frightened me. The pupils were too big. What had he seen, this athlete? What horrors? 'I ran out of the Dark,' he said, 'just like I ran into it. It's everywhere and nowhere.' With his free hand he reached up and touched my forehead. His fingertips were ice-cold. 'It's in here.'

I stared into his eyes, searching for a sign that he was telling the truth.

'Now go,' he said, withdrawing his arms and curling up on the bed.

'Gledhill.' It was my turn to grab hold of him. 'How do I get there?' I hissed.

He turned and lay on his back again. 'Go out of the Secure Unit and turn immediately left, then left again and you won't be far away.'

There was a sound behind me. Footsteps coming our way. Gledhill tensed and his head whipped around to watch the corner of the wall. I saw terror in his eyes and as I crawled around the back of his bed to hide I understood why they didn't need to put locks on his door. The man had been so profoundly frightened by something – whatever he saw in the Dark perhaps – that he no longer had the nerve to turn a simple corner.

A thin man in a white coat appeared. He had unruly eyebrows and wore glasses that were lopsided on his squashed face due to their missing arm. He reminded me of someone but I couldn't think who. I felt sick with fear and a growing sense of paranoia that I hadn't wanted to acknowledge. White Coat asked Gledhill if he was all right; he had heard voices.

'Dreams,' said Gledhill. 'I was having dreams.'

'Well, keep it down. You're disturbing the other patients.'

With that he was gone. I stood up and looked at Gledhill. 'Thank you,' I said. 'I'll go now.' He didn't speak. I touched his cold hand briefly, which elicited no response, and then I walked around the corner.

The long ward was as before. No sign of White Coat. I walked to the end and, as Gledhill had reluctantly advised, turned left and left again. I was in another long corridor, this time darker and seeming to dip as it went. I shivered and pulled my jacket tighter around me. I could hear something in the distance. Somebody moving furniture around or wheeling heavy trolleys on a resounding surface. Enough to make sweat bead on my forehead.

I reached a door with a small window. I looked into a white-shining lab. There was noise. People moving around, talking, rattling metal and glass things in sinks, but I couldn't see anyone, not even shadows. Then, I saw White Coat pass right by the little window. He was inches from me and would have seen me if he hadn't been looking down at something he was carrying. I didn't see what it was because I'd bobbed down out of sight. He must have been standing at the workbench just to the right of the door. I heard him walk back past the door and I moved away down the corridor. Only ten yards away the corridor came to an end. To the left was a fire-exit door with a push bar. Outside was a dark, empty courtyard. I had only to go through that door and I'd be out of immediate danger. Possibly there'd be a quick escape route out of the grounds. But Gledhill had put the idea in my head that somewhere down this corridor I'd find my way into the Dark. The fire exit didn't look that significant. I followed the corridor around to the right. A little way up was another door. I stepped through into a warm, stale, reeking ward and my flesh started to crawl.

The ward probably connected with White Coat's lab by an interconnecting door in the far right hand corner. I went the other way, towards the beds and the tiny muttering, chattering forms that moved under the blankets.

A bitter film coated the inside of my mouth. As I got nearer to the beds the noise of one pathetically abnormal voice chanting rose above all the other sounds: 'Two three, Two three... Two three, two three...'

I realised who White Coat reminded me of and stopped in the middle of ward, too frightened to go on, too far committed to go back.

'Two three, two three...'

I started walking again, sweat running down my back, sticking my shirt to my skin.

'Two three, two three. Two three, two three.'

There were at least a dozen beds. All the occupants were small children and all of them were strapped into place with leather restraints. They shifted their little bodies about but despite apparent strength could not loosen the straps. Their heads moved freely, swivelling at the neck. I wanted to free them but was too scared to attempt to do so. They had been strapped down for a reason, after all. The bed I was approaching was the first one on the left hand side of the ward.

'Two three, Two three.'

The boy's head, twisting from side to side on the bolster, was covered in a fine layer of dark brown hair. It was lighter under the eyes and around the mouth, where the pink skin showed through more clearly. His small ears were flattened against the side of his head and he had no lips. His eyes were very nearly those of a healthy, normal boy. There was intelligence in them but it was in their accentuated roundedness that you could see most clearly the canine influence. In the eyes and the mouth, which jutted subtly like a sculptor's failed attempt at a snout.

The child was trying to count. But because of his deformed mouth he couldn't manage to round the 'O' to say *one* and the lack of lips prevented him pronouncing *four*. So he went no further than *two three*.

This was what I was thinking as I watched him, my throat constricted by a lump, my stomach tying itself in knots. Anything to occupy the mind while I beheld the atrocity. It turned out I was wrong. As I backed away I saw the clipboard hooked on the end of the bed. The chart was headed with the patient's number: 2323.

The boy was proclaiming his identity. He wanted people to know who he was. I wondered what kind of awareness he had of *what* he was.

The other beds held little boys – and two girls – all in different stages of development. Some appeared to have more dog in them than others. 2323 was one of the most human-looking. None of the others spoke their number like 2323. Some uttered gibberish, a few could only manage certain vowel sounds. Others barked and yelped.

I stood over the first boy's bed. His head whipped from side to side like a metronome. With shaking fingers I reached forward and drew the sheet back an inch or two. There were straps under the covers as well. One chafed at his neck. It was red and sore. I couldn't bear it any longer. When I looked into his eyes it was like meeting the stare of the bed-ridden man in the flashlit, blood-stained house – the man who looked like me.

'Two three, two three.'

The Thin Controller had always spoken a call-sign twice. I was always *Two Three, Two Three*, never just *Two Three*.

The head beat hard against the pillow. A thread of saliva flew out of his mouth. And he kept on repeating his number, his name. I reached under the covers and undid the buckle on his leather neck restraint. His head shot upwards, checked again by straps lower down, and it jerked violently from side to side.

I heard a noise and whirled around. The ward behind me had become as dark as a forest in the thick of night, impenetrable. I turned back to the poor twisting creature in the bed but he'd gone too. Where his bed had been there was just blackness.

Vivid colours flashed in my head and formed into tiny fish swimming in the night's endless sea. They darted one way then shimmied back on themselves in a vast shoal and vanished. In turn I felt giddy, sick, weightless and afraid. Helpless and very small. Alone, completely alone in the night.

I WENT WITH my mother and father to visit relatives on the coast. I called them Uncle Billy and Auntie Nan but in actual fact they weren't family. Uncle Billy had worked with my father's uncle on the fishing boats and Billy and Nan had become such close family friends that they were always Aunt and Uncle to me.

They kept a dog.

We were sitting in the front room having a cup of tea and some fruit shortcake biscuits, my mother and father talking animatedly with Uncle Billy and Auntie Nan while I sat back on the settee eyeing the white Staffordshire bull terrier. I wouldn't have stared, only it was looking right at me and I was scared to look away. I imagined it coming for me, snapping and biting, and the four of them just carrying on their conversation. Or they'd turn and laugh, thinking the dog was playing with me. Uncle Billy wouldn't call the dog off until it had drawn my blood.

I could hear my heart beating and the dog, no doubt able to smell my fear, beat its tail on the hearth rug.

My mother looked at me and smiled. 'Are you all right, pet?' she said, then turned away because Auntie Nan had asked her something.

They won't help you, the dog seemed to be saying with its sinister, too-small brown eyes.

Later, they were all outside admiring the clematis that climbed over the shed at the bottom of the garden. The dog was with them, basking on the lawn. I was bored and wandered from room to room, ending up in my Aunt and Uncle's bedroom upstairs. I looked out of the window, saw the four grown-ups in a small group by a flower bed. The dog looked up and met my stare. I dropped down out of sight, sweat pricking the back of my neck. With no real awareness of what I was doing I began to open and close the drawers in my Aunt's dressing table, not really seeing anything, just handling things and putting them back and closing the drawer.

I heard a noise behind me and I stiffened. In the dressing table mirror I saw the white dog standing erect, ears sticking up, in the doorway. I jumped when it barked. Too frightened to turn around and face it, I watched in the mirror as it padded into the bedroom. Only when it barked again and broke into a run did I react, scrambling up to stand on the stool. But I was still within easy reach of the dog. It barked and barked, terrifyingly loud in the enclosed space, and I clambered onto the dressing table itself, my feet slipping on my Auntie's clothes, things I'd unconsciously removed from the drawers. The dog leaped at my feet, saliva spraying from its hot snapping mouth. I skipped sideways, screaming, backing onto the window ledge. But my left leg caught the edge of the mirror and I fell, knocking my shin against the edge of the dressing table and landing on the floor at the dog's feet.

It was on me in a second, fixing its jaws around my upper arm and pulling at me, as if to goad me into a fight. The foul stink of the animal made me retch, its hot breath curled up my nose like a poison and its teeth sank deeper into my arm. I screamed and yelled. In desperation I fought back, no longer caring that to do so would enrage the beast. I kicked and beat the dog with my free hand, but its jaws were clamped tightly around my arm.

I felt a wave of black giddiness wash over me, saw sparks dance in front of my eyes. I wet myself and my limbs went momentarily slack. The dog pressed one of its sharp-nailed feet on my chest, slipping to my throat. Just when I had completely given up the fight and thought I was about to faint my father appeared in the doorway, howling like a warrior as he threw himself at the dog. His sheer weight knocked the animal off me and he rolled with it on the floor. My Auntie Nan gathered me into her arms. I yelled, screaming and crying. Then my father was standing up, holding the dog's two front legs. He'd forced the legs apart and looked about ready to tear the dog right open down its seam. He was panting, bleeding from a cut on his cheek, looking at us and at my Mother and Uncle Billy who had just made it upstairs. My mother screamed when she saw my father. I wriggled out of Auntie Nan's embrace and crashed into my mother's legs. She hugged me fiercely, saying 'It's all right, Carl. It's all right, love,' over and over again.

Uncle Billy snapped the dog's lead onto its collar and took it from my father, who collapsed on the edge of the bed. I watched him, my chest still heaving. For a few minutes everyone maintained the same positions and no one spoke. I knew how weak the treatment had made my father, yet he had fought with the dog as if it were the sickness itself. And won.

Two days later I came home from the recreation ground. I'd been kicking a ball around with some friends. After the visit to Maine Road I now imagined myself as Francis Lee or Colin Bell as I took pot shots at Dave Enty who stood like some gloved statue between the two piles of coats we used as posts.

I walked past the garage and entered the house by the side door. I called out but no answer came. On the dining table there was a note from my mother. She'd gone shopping and would be back about five. I looked at my watch. It was half past three. I wondered why the side door had been unlocked. My father had gone to Christie's around twelve and I'd gone out to play football before he'd come back.

I took off my muddy trainers and walked upstairs in my stocking feet. My parents' bedroom was empty, the bed all made and everything very neat as usual, looking like a show house. In my own room I sat on the edge of the bed and flicked a half-made pampas-grass quill float that was standing in a jam jar on my desk. My father had made the desk for me. I opened its single drawer and shuffled through my Esso World Cup coins, Brooke Bond tea cards and old bus tickets. I stood up and looked out of the window to see if I could see my father coming back from the railway station.

There was something wrong. I knew it in my stomach first, where some sort of bitter fight was going on.

I went in the bathroom to see if I could resolve the dispute but nothing came. I washed my hands, a little unnerved by the sound of the running water, which seemed too loud for the emptiness of the house. Downstairs I turned the television on and glanced at the different channels. I thumbed the off switch and stood at the window looking out at the garage. Something gnawed at my insides.

Leaves were falling outside. There had been a subtle smoky taste in the air that I'd noticed coming back from the rec. The first bonfires of the season were being lit in gardens. Down back entries kids were sneaking the last illicit cigarettes of the summer holidays.

I wandered into the kitchen and pulled open the fridge door. There wasn't much: some butter and milk, rashers of bacon wrapped in foil, and a hunk of cheese. I closed the fridge and hovered by the side door leading back outside. Through the frosted glass I could see the distorted form of the garage. I put my muddy trainers back on and opened the door. Going left, I walked down the passage between the garage and the back garden. There was a peculiar smell coming from somewhere that set my teeth on edge. And a low growling noise I couldn't identify. I trailed my fingers against the side of the garage and slipped around the corner at its end. There was a mossy tree stump which I had to stand on to look through the grimy window in the back wall of the garage.

At first it was difficult to see clearly because of the two thicknesses of glass and the dirty swirling clouds of some kind of smoke. But eventually the details resolved themselves and made sense.

The car was in the garage and my father was sitting in the driving seat.

His head was moving from side to side, his mouth gaping open and snapping shut. His eyes met mine.

I stared at him for a few elastic seconds then dropped down off the mossy stump and sat in the soil at the base of the garage wall. I was panting for breath, my heart hammering, pulse racing in my temples. Sweat in a sheen across my forehead making me shiver. My hands shaking.

But I didn't get up and run to open the garage door. There was still time, I knew, because he had been moving. He had seen me.

I turned around and pressed my ear to the side of the garage. I heard the low rumbling of the car's engine, the chugging of the exhaust. The smell was sickening.

I got up and ran. I ran down the passage between the house and the garage and straight out into the road. A car slammed on its brakes, squealing to a standstill. The driver thumped his horn. Burning rubber stung my nostrils. I ran over the road and dived into the nearest back entry, the damp cobbles slippery under my feet. At the corner I bowled into someone coming the other way. Without looking to see who it was I picked myself up and carried on running.

I ran for about two miles until I simply couldn't go another step and I collapsed on the canal tow path in a tangle of long dewy grass and dead broken branches. I buried my head and cried until it hurt. Soon the longed-for oblivion came and I blacked out.

A white-haired man out walking his dog found me and took me to the nearby police station because he couldn't get any sense out of me. They took me home. I eyed the flung-open garage doors with terror. My mother had found him. I hadn't warned her. I hadn't done the one thing my father would have wanted me to do.

The engine had stopped because it had run out of petrol. Despite the open doors there was still a nauseating stench. The policemen covered their faces with handkerchiefs before picking their way past the lawnmower and gardening implements.

There was a length of garden hose running from the exhaust pipe into the car via the back window, which was still wound up almost to the top. The driver's door was open and my father's blackened hand hung out of it. I didn't get to see his face again because a policeman turned me around and led me outside. We found my mother in the back garden tearing clumps of bindweed out of the earth. One of the policemen approached from the side very carefully and reached out to touch her shoulder. She twisted away from him and raked her fingers through the soil, digging up more strands of bindweed. The trouble had always been that no matter how many individual strands she pulled up, the roots remained. It always grew back.

The policeman tried to get a grip and she snapped her arm like a whip, showering him with soil and grit. Then she saw me standing there with the other policeman and that was when she started screaming.

I FELT MYSELF moving slowly, rising through clouds of black, star-flecked matter towards a glimmer of light that grew dimmer as I neared it. My body felt paradoxically weightless and tethered; either way I had little control over it. The sounds of small dogs and children playing together in some distant park seemed like a trick of memory.

I woke up in the children's ward, a bare bulb dispensing a sickly yellowish glow above the end of my bed. When I tried to sit up I found myself unable to. I had been strapped in like the crossbreed children in the beds on my left and opposite. Next to my bed sitting upright with his legs crossed and wearing a white coat was Gledhill.

I gave up struggling against the straps and lay back. For the time being the runaway train that was my escape from the City had been shunted into a siding.

The Gledhill thing didn't dismay me as much as it might have done; I was merely puzzled as to who was betraying me this time. Was it Stella? And had she set up the trap at Maxi's dental surgery? Or had Stella been telling what she believed was the truth when she passed on the name of Gledhill? Had the authorities somehow received intelligence that I was coming looking for the ex-Dark wanderer?

For now, Gledhill just sat and watched me. I wondered what his brief was. Guard or professional observer? I heard footsteps approaching the bed. It was White Coat, eyebrows twitching. He exchanged a few words quietly with Gledhill then stepped closer to the bed and loomed over me.

'How's our King killer then?' he asked sarcastically. 'Enjoy your little sojourn in the Dark, did you?'

I hesitated for a moment. I had been waiting a long time for this, since the first time I encountered the Thin Controller.

'Cunt.'

'Security are on their way. You'll soon change your tune then,' he said. 'This isn't a fucking holiday camp, you know.'

I thought about answering him back but there was no point. I'd made my gambit.

'In the meantime,' he continued, 'we are responsible for your comfort.' He turned half an inch in Gledhill's direction. 'Make sure he's comfortable please, Doctor Gledhill.' With that he turned and walked out of my field of vision. Gledhill got up from his seat. The paralysed look to the left side of his face had not been an act, though in this new context it twisted his mouth into a snarl.

He bent down and I felt him grab hold of something and pull. The broad leather strap across my chest tightened and I gasped for air. He tugged on the other straps that restrained my arms and legs and I made no show of resistance. There was no point at this stage. I closed my eyes but although sleep beckoned I didn't want to be sucked back into the Dark.

I had an idea and turned to face Gledhill.

'I want to make a telephone call,' I said.

He appeared unmoved by my request.

'You have to allow me a phone call, Doctor,' I pressed him. 'Ask *him* if you have to.'

He got up and walked over to the door in the far corner. I was left alone with the crossbreeds whose cacophony continued unabated. After some minutes Gledhill reappeared wheeling a trolley. White Coat was two steps behind him. Gledhill brought the trolley to the side of my bed. An old-fashioned black telephone sat on it. There was a long flex which Gledhill bent down to plug in behind the bed. He lifted the handset and, finger poised, looked at me.

'Number?' he said.

'I'll do it myself.'

Gledhill looked at White Coat, who signalled his assent. The necessary straps were loosened and I took the telephone down from the trolley, dialling the first few digits of Annie Risk's number quickly and in the shadow of the trolley so they couldn't follow it. I heard the ringing tone at the other end and swopped the phone over to the left side of the bed. White Coat and Gledhill stayed where they were. The ringing tone ceased and I heard Annie's voice through a squizzle of interference.

'Hello?'

'Can you hear me?' I said.

'Hello?'

I tried again, shouting, but she couldn't hear.

'I can't hear anything,' she said and was silent for a moment, then: 'Carl, is that you?'

'Yes,' I shouted.

'Carl, if that's you' – her voice sounded anxious – 'come back, you've got to get back. We're in terrible trouble. Awful things are happening. People are disappearing. You've got to come back. Come back and help us, Carl. We need you.'

'I'm coming, I'm coming.'

The line went dead. Gledhill stood up straight, the plug dangling from his hand.

'She can't hear you, King killer,' White Coat said with a sneer. 'You can hear them but they can't hear you. That's how it works. All those wrong numbers you used to get, picking up the phone and there's no one there, that's people calling out of the City. Just to listen to your confused babble because they know you won't be able to hear them. Or maybe like you they want to ask for help, but they soon realise there's no escape, and what links there are only go one way.

'She's right though,' he continued. 'Terrible things are happening over there. Our influence is spreading thanks to you.'

I frowned.

'Yes, you, assassin,' he said. 'Our agents of darkness are slipping through into your world via the gap you so conveniently left in the side of the City when you walked in off the motorway.'

'Your lot have been around in our world longer than that,' I said, remembering what Stella had told me – how she was snatched from beside the railway line on her way home after jumping a quintuple salchow at the local rink.

'But we could only maintain a small presence and only along the canals and railways and in the grey areas,' said Gledhill, clearly getting over-enthusiastic. White Coat cracked a sharp look at him that caused him to shut up and withdraw like a whipped dog.

'What he means,' White Coat said, taking up the story, 'is that now we can put more ambitious campaigns into action. All thanks to you. Your friend was right: people are disappearing. We have infiltrated the police and their dog handlers with some of our own security and our own dogs. Well, you can imagine the rest.'

White Coat was getting into his stride. He had never seemed happy with his lot in our world as the Thin Controller. Over here agreed with him. I was going to enjoy dispatching him when the time came.

The grimace slid off his face as the door swung open and a security outfit bustled in. They came to the end of the bed and the goon in charge muttered an exchange with White Coat while Gledhill released my bonds. I stretched, cracking my joints, and stood up.

'You could have taken my boots off,' I remarked to Gledhill.

White Coat left the room by the door in the far corner and I barely had time to glance at the faces and dark uniforms of the goon squad before he came back with an upright bed base which he pushed along the floor on castors. There were leather hoops at the four corners of the frame and three broad straps flapping loose across its width. White Coat parked it in the middle of the ward and two of the guards dragged me across. I was strapped in place, my body assuming the X position. What was coming next? Why these elaborate preparations? I felt an uncomfortable piece of apparatus descending over my head and White Coat himself affixed four sets of pincers that were attached to it onto my eyelids to prevent them from closing. Then he signalled to Gledhill, who drew a plastic bottle from his pocket and approached me.

'No,' I cried. 'No, no.'

'But you don't know what we're going to do, King killer,' White Coat sneered.

One of the soldiers lit a cigarette and I imagined them burning me with it.

Gledhill opened his plastic bottle and pulled out a pipette. He reached up to my eye. I couldn't close it, though I tried and the pain cut through my face like a knife. He squeezed the rubber bulb on the pipette and a drop of liquid fell into my eye.

'Don't worry, King killer, it's only water,' Gledhill said. 'We've got something to show you.' He moistened my other eye. 'We want you to have a good view.'

There was a commotion at the far end of the ward. The doors swung inwards and a party of soldiers entered. They had three prisoners. One man was frog-marched between the beds until he was only two feet from me. Soldiers held his arms while he struggled like a child. His wide, staring blue eyes pierced mine.

'Wolf,' I said.

Tears fell from his eyes. They ran into the greasy stubble covering his pinched cheeks. The two soldiers drew him back from me and White Coat stepped forward, followed by another soldier carrying a steel poker. The heat coming off its red tip caused distortion in the air.

'You see, King killer,' White Coat said, 'we are humane here in the City. We don't like to see people suffer and your friend has been suffering ever since he went into the Dark. He must have seen such terrible things and he's still seeing them now.'

I understood at last the reason for his awful stare, although I would never know what he'd seen in the dark. 'Let him go,' I pleaded.

For all my suspicions at the time, Wolf and his colleagues had been on my side. I could see the dark form of Giff and the rake-like Professor bound by chains among the soldiers at the far end.

'Let them go. I'm the one you want.'

But White Coat had stepped aside to let the soldier with the poker stand in between Wolf and me.

'We don't want him to suffer these sights any longer,' White Coat said, and the soldier lifted the poker. From Wolf's open mouth came a scream so high-pitched and ragged I thought it would rip apart my eardrums. Soldiers held his head so that he couldn't dodge the attack. I heard a terrible fizzling as the poker put out his left eye. Matter and fluid spat outwards, striking the soldier's uniform. Still Wolf screamed. The soldier withdrew his poker before it lost all its heat to one socket. Gledhill continued to drip water into my eyes so that I could see clearly. I cursed him and all of them. The poker sank into Wolf's other eye and I saw his knees begin to buckle as the eye boiled and sputtered before slumping misshapen down his cheek.

I thought the show was over but I was wrong. Another frame similar to my own was wheeled in and Wolf lifted onto it. Once Wolf had been secured, White Coat stepped forward with a scalpel in his hand.

'Stop,' I shouted.

But White Coat took no notice as he cut off Wolf's sleeve and twisted a tourniquet around his upper arm. Wolf stirred and moaned. The soldiers tightened his bindings and White Coat sliced into Wolf's forearm, opening a gash three inches long and deep to the bone. A soldier staunched the flow of blood with a rolled-up length of torn bed sheet. White Coat reached around the soldier to get something from a trolley. It was a thin but strong-looking length of plaited leather, like a lead.

Gledhill's face hovered beneath mine as he dripped more water into my eyes.

White Coat threaded the leather strap under the bone and tied it there. He tugged on it and Wolf's screams became shriller. Happy, White Coat pressed the two sides of the forearm together, his ungloved thumbs slipping on the raw flesh and bloody skin, and with a needle handed to him he stitched up the incision.

He turned and looked at me. Gledhill watered my eyes. The leather strap dangled out of Wolf's arm, a steel ring glinting in the loop at its end.

One of the soldiers snapped his fingers and the doors were pushed open again. A dog handler entered, pulled along the tiled floor by a dark brown pit bull, snarling and spitting. Behind me the children and little creatures started up their howling, yelping chorus again. The soldier unclasped the pit bull's lead from his chain and fastened it to the lead that emerged from the wound in Wolf's arm.

The dog strained at the new lead. It tore open two of White Coat's stitches before the soldiers were able to undo all of the hoops and straps holding the all-but-broken man. Once Wolf was free, the dog pulled him to the floor. He managed to stand up but the dog raced down the ward and the blind man fell headlong, hitting his head against the end of a bed. Two soldiers picked him up and let his guide dog drag him screaming from the ward. His screams echoed down the corridor as the pit bull led him away into the night.

The goons released me and marched me off past White Coat, who watched with bloody-sleeved arms folded across his chest, and past the soldiers holding Giff and the Professor, who stared through me at the prospect of their own fate.

'Don't worry, fellas. None of this is real,' I said to them. 'This is not happening.'

'You tell yourself that,' said White Coat.

Before we left the ward, one of the soldiers pulled my hands behind my back and secured them with a plastic grip that dug into my wrists. My legs were cracked repeatedly with a baton as I was pushed along in the middle of the group. A black van stood waiting in a floodlit courtyard. I was bundled in and we left the hospital grounds by the main gate. I had to sit on the floor in the back of the van and when we went around corners I rolled over, banging my head. One of the goons leaned across and poked me with his baton.

'Keep still, King killer,' he spat.

I said nothing and was sick in the corner. I wondered about what I'd said to Giff and the Professor. I asked myself where the impulse to say that had come from.

The van jerked and the engine was killed. The guards jumped out and I heard their boots scrunch on grit as they came around to unlock the back doors.

'I guess you'll have a jeering crowd ready out there,' I said to them. 'A braying mob.'

They dragged me out of the van and missiles and abuse rained down on me from all sides.

'What did I tell you?' I said.

The guards frogmarched me into the back of some building. I was expecting a gaol cell but it soon became apparent that it was to the law courts that they had brought me. Within three minutes I was standing in the dock, my hands still bound behind my back and my ankles fastened together by a chain. A chorus rang out from the public gallery – 'King killer, King killer, King killer!' Things were moving much faster than I had anticipated.

Chapter Thirteen

THE CHARGE WAS regicide.

Specifically that I had planned and executed the assassination of the King by a single shot from a rifle while he was being driven through the City in his car on official duties.

There was a row of people sitting in a box marked Prosecution Witnesses. I'd never seen any of them before. There was no box of defence witnesses, no defence lawyer as far as I could see, just a barrage of prosecution lawyers and the judge, all of whom had spiral scars scratched on their foreheads.

The clerk of the court was already reading out special clauses that meant nothing to me. The prosecution counsel stood up and declaimed from his little podium. I had killed the King. These witnesses had seen me do it. The penalty was death. I should be taken from this court...

The proceedings seemed to be running away from me at an implausible speed. If I failed to intervene, the whole thing would be over without my having spoken a word.

'Stop!' I ordered. The courtroom fell quiet and everyone stared at me. Rows and rows of blank faces that seemed to extend beyond the natural confines of the room. In the public gallery I caught sight of Stella sitting just in front of Maxi. White Coat, cleaned up, and Gledhill were standing to one side by the exit doors, behind a cordon of policemen armed with batons. Everyone held their breath waiting for me to speak again.

I looked at the judge. He was dressed like his street-corner peers in a tight-fitting shiny black suit. The scar on his forehead caught a slanting ray of light from the windows high up in the courtroom wall.

'What's he doing?' I asked, pointing at a burly man wearing headphones and bending over a cutting lathe. There was an acetate disc in position on his turntable.

'Recording the proceedings,' said the clerk of the court.

'I'm speaking to the judge,' I thundered, finding confidence from somewhere.

The judge himself spoke: 'As the clerk said, the case is being recorded.'

I knew what would be on the disc when the verdict had been delivered and the condemned man taken away: forty-five minutes of silence. Ticks, hisses, booms and clicks but no witness testimonies, no impassioned plea of defence.

So, I had to win the case first time around. There could be no appeal.

'Continue,' said the judge with a vague hand gesture in the direction of the prosecution counsel.

The arrogant young lawyer picked up a book from the table in front of him.

'This book,' he said, brandishing what appeared to be my copy of *Un Régicide* at the court, 'was found in the possession of the accused. As evidence linking him to the crime for which he stands accused it is damning.'

'Stop,' I cried again. 'I want to speak.'

This seemed to take everyone by surprise. There was a collective rustle as all the figures in the courtroom turned towards me again. Row upon row of blank faces.

'I don't have a defence counsel so I'm going to defend myself.' I looked around the court. No one spoke or moved. In the public gallery I glimpsed my mother's face and my stomach turned over, but when I looked back she wasn't there. It was just some anonymous bloodless face like a rolled-out lump of pastry. Could have been anybody. 'I didn't shoot the King…' I began again before being interrupted.

'Objection, Your Honour,' said the prosecutor. 'The accused did commit the offence. That is established fact.'

'Objection sustained,' the judge muttered.

I couldn't believe my ears. 'Objection,' I shouted. 'It is not fact. You will hear the facts now.' Suddenly, despite my weak position and my physical restraints I felt I was in a position of power. Despite a ruling from the judge the prosecutor had fallen silent – his head was bowed over his desk – and the assembly was turned my way again.

'To begin with, I did not kill the King. I have never owned a rifle and nor did I ever see the King being driven through the City.' I looked around at my audience. The numbers in the public gallery had swelled and my mother's face was once more amongst them. I felt encouraged. If she blamed me for what had happened, not only for the death of my father but also for what it had done to her, would she not be sitting in the prosecution witness box rather than the public gallery?

The court was hushed, waiting for me to continue. The prosecutor appeared to have frozen to the spot. Only the cutting engineer's disc moved, producing a low hiss. I sensed the need to go further.

'The King was dying. He was suffering from a terminal condition which he knew would continue to cause him more and more pain and discomfort the longer he lived. He debated with himself the rights and wrongs of taking his own life and reached the decision that it would be better to do so. What right did I have to alter that decision at the last moment?'

A broad band of pain stretched across the front of my skull. Sweat tickled my neck and ran down my back. I couldn't massage my temples or run a handkerchief over my face for even temporary relief. When I looked up at the public gallery it seemed impossibly distant, as if viewed down the wrong end of a telescope. My head started to spin. I looked at the prosecution witness box and it seemed as if its occupants had swopped positions with each other, but I couldn't be sure. The prosecutor still stood with his head bowed. The judge had turned his head to bathe his face in the light streaming in from the high window.

'I didn't kill the King,' I repeated. 'He killed himself. I just let him do it. In the circumstances it was the right and most humane thing to do.'

In the public gallery my mother's head was nodding slowly like a huge white bell. It was the only movement in the entire courtroom.

'It was the right thing to do,' I repeated.

If I really believed it, however, why when I looked back at the judge did I see my father's face swinging from side to side behind the windscreen of his exhaust-clogged car? I blinked and shook my head and when I looked again I saw the judge shaking his head slowly and making an ambiguous gesture with his hand. The prosecutor, upon seeing this sign, slipped back to life, along with the rest of the court. It was like a piece of film that had been stuck in the gate of the projector slowly being freed and rolling again. The sound slurred back up to the correct speed and full volume. Witnesses stood up one after another in the prosecution witness box and rattled off accounts of how they had seen me holding the rifle, training its sights on the car that was carrying the King, squeezing the trigger. They saw the rear passenger window of the car shatter and the King slump forward inside. They saw me run away from the scene of the crime and collapse on the tow path of one of the City's canals.

'No, no,' I shouted. 'None of this is true. It's not true. I didn't kill him.'

I looked at the last witness, the one who'd seen me on the canal bank. He was a middle-aged man with white hair. I just bet he kept a dog as well. The prosecutor was summing up. All was quiet in the public gallery; my mother had disappeared. The judge laid his right arm across his own chest then pointed at my head. I looked up at the bright window and heard the judge's gavel crash onto the leather stopper on his desk and suddenly the courtroom was in uproar. Officers freed my ankles and pushed me out of the dock. The crowd on the floor of the court parted to let us through. Bystanders and court officials shouted insults and spat at me as guards prodded and kicked me out into the open air where a mass of people had already gathered. They chanted 'King killer, King killer' and moved with the awesome, graceful give-and-take of the sea.

I was dragged up onto the back of a trailer and the tailgate was bolted after me. Four guards shared the trailer with me, each armed with a baton and an old-fashioned rifle. A sixth person – a woman – was helped up into the trailer as it began to move off through the crowds. When the woman turned around I saw it was Maxi. She was holding a straight razor in her right hand. My chest tightened and my throat dried. However poor the prospects for survival, the promise of pain is never easy to bear. Hence a dying man's desire to commit suicide.

While the guards concentrated on the crowd so they could avert any attempt to kill me before the appointed time, Maxi set about finishing off the haircut she had started. Although a double-crosser, she was at least a familiar face.

'Where are we going?' I asked her as she grasped a handful of my hair and sliced cleanly through it. The razor was so sharp it almost wasn't there.

'You know where we're going,' she whispered.

'How do they do it?' I asked.

'They have different ways.'

Part of me believed there had to be a way out. With my hands still secured by the plastic tie, however, it was going to be difficult. A stone thrown from the crowd hit me on the leg and my sudden movement caused Maxi to nick my scalp. It was so hot and sharp I didn't realise until I felt the warm trickle of blood – stickier and thicker than sweat – make its way down past my ear. One of the guards fired over the crowd.

'What about afterwards?' I asked.

'What do you mean, afterwards?' she hissed. 'There is no afterwards. This is it. The big one.'

'Do I get buried, eaten by dogs, or what?'

She didn't answer, just carried on shaving my head. I could tell she was being careful to avoid cutting me.

'So?' I insisted.

'You know this place,' she said mysteriously.

'What do you mean?'

'Hey, King killer!' It was one of the guards. He thumped my shoulder with the butt of his rifle. 'Shut the fuck up.'

The trailer rumbled on and eventually the guard had to turn his attention back to the mob below. Fists shaking, eyes rolling, they kept up their tirade of abuse.

'They've systematically been slaughtering suspects here for years,' Maxi continued. 'But this place doesn't follow your rules. The dead won't lie down.'

'They can't kill me?' I said.

'They can kill you. And they will. But you won't lie down and be buried.'

She fell silent, chopping away at what was left of my hair. I watched it fall to the floor of the trailer, hoping I would get a chance to grow it again. I wondered if they'd let me have a last cigarette. I still had a couple of Camels down my left boot, if they weren't squashed beyond smoking by now.

'I was reading a book before I came here,' I told her, 'in which the action constantly switched between two worlds. In one of them, the king was due to be assassinated, but then his body turned up in the other. And although one thread featured an unnamed first-person narrator and the other a protagonist called Boris, you sensed they were the same person. I wish I could just switch back to the other world like Boris could.'

'Be careful what you wish for,' she said in a whisper. 'That's what they're going to do. Take you into your world. As the train crosses over, the dead lie down.'

'What train? And then what? Do they bring the bodies back?'

'No. If they did so, they'd just get up again. It's that kind of place.' She dragged the dry razor over the dome of my head, now almost bald. 'They leave them there. In your world.'

The trailer was pulled off the main road into a grid of short straight side streets. The crowd was no longer stationary. Thousands of people were streaming through the streets alongside us, hundreds more joining the flow from other streets and back entries. I knew where we were going. There hadn't been any sign of a football stadium on my map but I didn't doubt that was where we were heading. I didn't have long. There had to be some break in the network of streets. I needed another element. I needed an escape route. My eyes searched the back streets and patches of waste ground, searching for the interstices.

There had to be one somewhere. It should be part of the geography of this part of the City. Every urban area had its grey area on the edge of the inner city. Derelict housing, old warehouses, dead industry, waste land, football grounds, railway sidings, gasholders, canals. Brownfield sites, interzones, edgelands.

I pictured the football ground. I imagined the splash of green under the floodlights. I imagined being led to the middle of the pitch – and then what? Would there be a gibbet? A trapdoor? A guillotine? A simple post and a firing squad?

Then I saw what I wanted, glinting like a seam of jet in redundant rock. A narrow, oil-black canal threading its way between the backs of two streets. The street we were on would go over it in fifty yards or so. Not a bridge as such, the width of the canal hardly merited it, but there was just a chance. In my position the slightest chance was worth taking. If I fell to my death at least I would have chosen the manner of my going, which was preferable to whatever execution the authorities had planned for me in the stadium.

Right at the last moment the truck that was pulling the trailer seemed about to turn off into another street away from the canal. My mouth filled with the acid taste of fear. But the truck bumped onwards. I looked at the guards. They were watching the flow of humanity in the streets. The trailer was drawn past the last row of houses before the canal and past the back entry whose cobbles shone in the orange light like fat little fish. I jumped.

In the air my arms came free. The plastic tie had been cut clean through. Only a razor would have produced such a clean cut. I didn't have time to protect my face or hold my nose before striking the water. It went up my nostrils as I sank deeper and felt my leg hit the bottom. Thinking my head was about to burst I turned and headed under the road, swimming underwater. I couldn't open my eyes but I heard the bullets that tore through the water on either side of me. I dived deeper and swam along the bottom for as long as I could before I had to come up for air.

Despite the desperate need to empty my passages and breath fresh air I surfaced slowly and quietly.

I found myself in total darkness. I could hear a far-off rumble and clamour, the thump of my pulse, and a constant drip, presumably from the ceiling of the tunnel. I cleared my throat, took a few deep breaths and swam on. The taste of the canal water in my mouth was bitter and nauseating. My boots were slowing me down but if I got rid of them I knew I'd regret it later. I put everything into moving my arms and legs, thrusting forward and pushing water behind me, kicking back as if there *were* dogs snapping at my heels. Just when I was beginning to think I couldn't swim another stroke, I saw light up ahead. I listened but couldn't hear anything apart from my own echoing splashes.

Even with the tunnel exit in sight it was the cold that now got to me. My limbs felt as if they had been packed in ice and I had started to shiver violently. I forced myself on by willpower, thinking of Annie Risk. If she was in danger I had to get back for her sake as well as mine. The distraction of her image gave me a few more strokes.

Ten yards from the end of the tunnel, I dived and swam as far as I could, then veered to the left-hand side and broke the surface. Water dripped off my nose.

The tow path and nearby streets were empty. I clambered out and sat on the bank, taking off my boots and emptying them. A minute later I set off again, trotting along the tow path, looking for what I guessed I would come across sooner or later. Only two hundred yards further on I found what I wanted: a railway bridge. I climbed up the side and walked onto the line. Nothing was coming from either direction.

I had to choose: left or right. It wasn't quite fifty-fifty. My instinct said left because that way lay the stadium to which they had been taking me. Left would take me deep into the grey area where I would most likely find any sidings or depot. These wouldn't be far from the stadium, because of the difficulties of transporting the executed men from the football ground to the railway line without any of them escaping. To some extent I was busking it, making assumptions based on comments made by Gledhill – when he had talked of maintaining a presence in the grey areas along railway lines and canals – and Maxi, who had referred specifically to the dead lying down only when the train passed over into my world.

She had been on my side at the end, when it mattered, so I had to trust her information.

I shivered in the raw night air. The oily canal water was still making me slip as I skipped from sleeper to sleeper. The line was built on relatively high ground and I could see the City's lights spread out on the left. On the right lay darkness broken by a few scattered lamps. I was tempted to make off in that direction but resisted. I knew the City too well now to believe I might escape that way. The darkness would be thick with snares. I had come to understand that the City was everywhere and if you were inside the City looking out it stretched to infinity. If you were outside looking in, as I had been, it simply didn't exist in physical terms at all. Somehow it was everywhere and nowhere at the same time, as Gledhill-the-patient had said of the Dark.

I noticed movement in the streets on my left. At least a mile away lights were gathering around a central point. Then, as I continued running, they started to disperse in all directions, thousands of lights. People carrying flaming torches perhaps. Presumably curfew had been cancelled and all loyal citizens sent out to hunt me down. The thought lent speed to my flight. Some of the lights were heading for points further up the line. I had no choice but to continue running, convinced now that this was my last chance.

When I hit the sidings the lights were still half a mile away, bobbing and converging as they narrowed the gap. I listened hard and heard what I wanted – the chug-chug of an engine ticking over. The smells of diesel and grease were sweet after the foul stench of the canal. Floodlights positioned at the corners of the depot meant I had to proceed with more caution, but the engine noise was easy to locate. I picked my way over the tracks, ducking beneath lines of idle rolling stock and freight wagons. The velvety darkness beyond the sidings was dotted with coloured signals. The train with the live engine which I was now approaching appeared to be waiting for a red signal to go green. The locomotive was painted grey and red.

The wagons were old cattle trucks with wooden, slatted walls. I stopped by one and pressed my ear to the side. All I could hear was the persistent chugging of the diesel. I peered in between two vertical slats and what I saw made me look away and double up to be sick over the oily chippings.

In the semi-darkness of the wagon I'd seen ceiling-filtered light from the high floods falling across bare dirty-white thighs and torn shoulders, twisted, wasted arms and shaved heads.

These were the dead. And they were standing up.

The idle of the locomotive took on a different, higher tone. I looked up the line, vomit still burning the inside of my mouth, and the light flicked to green. The locomotive revved and a great cloud of diesel exhaust billowed into the floodlit night. The trucks were jerked into life in a long domino line and I reached for the catch on the gate. At first it wouldn't give and the loco gave its first real tug on the wagons. I had to jump and fiddle with the catch while walking sideways. Suddenly it fell open and I opened the gate just wide enough to squeeze in. I fastened it after me and stared out through the gaps in the truck wall at the receding lines of carriages and, jumping between them, the dancing flames of the late King's loyal avengers.

As a deathly chill spread from my stomach to claim my extremities and my heart pumped faster than the clickety-clack of the trucks on the track, I turned to face my companions.

Chapter Fourteen

THEIR EYES WERE open. The light in the truck was poor – narrow shafts admitted by the gaps in the walls – but sufficient to allow me glimpses of terrible wounds, encrusted with blood now cold and dark. No one had told me what form of execution was preferred in the City but many of the injuries were consistent with my suspicion that suspects had been thrown into the football ground to fight for their lives with vicious dogs.

A man propped up not two feet from me had a ragged hole in his throat where a beast's jaws had fastened and refused to let go. A short young man with a shock of blond curls and empty dark eyes had black puncture marks on his neck and chest. Either the accused were cast naked into the arena or the authorities stripped the bodies after the dogs had done their worst.

The train clattered on into the night, travelling distressingly slowly. I looked through a gap but couldn't see anything beyond the hedges and trees and occasional lights at the edge of the track.

There was a pungent smell in the truck, which I had been trying to ignore. All I could think of was the bag of turnips I had once left undisturbed for months in the crisper drawer of my fridge. When I came across it I took hold of the top of the bag and pulled. The paper bag, weakened by the soggy decaying mess inside, broke and decomposed vegetables went everywhere.

It was the details – the shaving scar, the mole on one woman's cheek, the pierced ears, dark roots amid dyed blonde hair – that affirmed the humanity of the train's cargo. Otherwise they could be sides of meat destined to hang on hooks in the market. And yet, though dead, they remembered enough of life to remain standing.

As the train slithered across a set of points the truck rocked and a tall man with a long, crumbling nose and a bloody superficial labyrinth where his right ear had been fell against me. I recoiled but he came with me, the weight of several bodies pushing him from behind. We tumbled to the floor of the truck. Bodies slithered over the tops of ones that had already fallen and soon I was buried beneath them, trying to block my nose and avert my gaze. Even when I thought the landslide had stopped, another slight jolt from the train scythed a fresh crop.

Winded and bruised I tried to crawl out from under the corpses and it suddenly occurred to me that the train must have crossed over into our world. That was why they had all fallen over. At last they could rest in peace.

But I realised I was wrong when I felt a tickling on my ankle and tried to pull it away and couldn't. One of the corpses was using it as a handhold and had started to climb up my body.

Another, a woman with a deep, sharp cleft in her face – the dull flesh of her cheek flapped loosely, exposing the glimmer of bone beneath, clearly not the work of pit bulls but that of a blade – approached me from my left. She crawled over the pile of bodies to get at me, clawing with her one good hand.

It dawned on me that I was the cause of these deaths. Or that was what the City would want me to think, anyway.

More of them found the energy to move, raising shaved heads that bore deep scratches from doing battle in the stadium, moving forward on elbows and stumps. Their desperate, vengeful hands reached out to my face, their broken, bone-splintered fingers cracking as they sought to put out my eyes, tear my flesh, as theirs had been.

I retreated into the corner, desperate to deflect their clumsy assaults. Still they came. As they hit me, some of them sacrificed their skin as it split from knuckle and joint like rotten fruit. The tall man with the crumbling nose had hauled himself up the length of my body and had his face next to mine. As weak blows landed on my legs and feet, this man opened his mouth as if to kiss out my life. His teeth were still good but his gums were rotting, his mouth having become a still-warm nest for fat white maggots, and the foul stench almost overpowered me. I was sick again, spitting bile at the man's face, into his glassy eyes.

He opened his mouth wider and several of the larvae tipped out, wriggling, falling down the front of my shirt. He was pressing closer to meet my lips when his head fell forward and thumped against my breastbone. I noticed the others collapsing. Their little attacks ceased and they rolled off me. I pushed the tall man away and the maggots spilled out of his mouth onto the floor of the wagon. I approached the side of the truck and peered out.

I saw a galaxy of red lights hanging seemingly in mid-air and wondered if instead of crossing back into the real world I had entered some even more bizarre territory. But as my eyes grew accustomed to the darkness I could make out vertical masts and diagonal stays. The lights were attached to the masts, which occupied a vast area on the right of the line. There was a road also. A vague memory plucked at the back of my mind. I'd seen the masts before.

It came to me: Rugby radio masts. If that were the case, the train would be pulling into Rugby station any minute. I opened the catch on the gate and made a wider crack in the side of the wagon. I craned my neck to see up the line. I could see lights and a station approaching.

I knew, however, that even if the train stopped or slowed down enough for me to jump, I wouldn't be able to. I might have seen no sign of them, but the train had to be carrying guards whose job it would be to unload the corpses. And if they didn't get me, I'd still be stuck in Rugby in the middle of the night.

I fastened the gate and crouched down as the train rumbled under the vast glass canopy of Rugby station. The platforms were lonely and wet but they were part of my world. I wanted to get out, bend down and kiss them. The train slowed down and stopped, presumably awaiting a green light. I watched through the cracks as a British Rail guard sauntered down the platform, tapping his whistle against the side of his leg. He stopped fifteen yards from my truck, took off his cap and smoothed his hand over his balding head, yawning. I wondered about trying to call him over but the train jerked into motion again and we trundled out of the station.

The train accelerated, heading north. It blasted through Coventry station without slowing down, skittered over the level crossings at Canley and Tile Hill, then raced through cuttings, a tunnel and more deep cuttings and another tiny station before easing off in the approach to Birmingham International. Even here, though, there was no command to halt and the train thundered on towards the heart of Birmingham, under one road, over the next, another level crossing, a blink of a station, more bridges and tunnels, long streets of houses rising on either side then falling away and cars suddenly passing beneath the moss-clad stone arches under the tracks. Through Stechford, and past a bleak ill-lit park on the right, and finally the driver applied the brakes. The cattle wagons rolled forward, under three more roads, past a works depot on the right. Less than a mile away M6 traffic whipped through a busy interchange. Amid a great clanking of iron and steel, the train halted.

In the sudden stillness I listened to the hum of the motorway and the stuttering hum of the diesel. In between the motorway and the railway were several gasholders, three of them bunched up close to the M6 – I'd passed them dozens of times driving up to Manchester – and two hemmed in between a canal on the left, a scraggy little river, the railway line where I was sitting, and another line which came out from underneath and veered off to the right.

Of these two gasholders – both were the spiral-guided design – one was full and the other still half-empty.

Why did I think of it as still half-empty rather than only half-full?

I heard movement on the line ahead; men jumping down to the chippings and walking down the track. I thought I knew what they were going to do, so I took my chance. It was risky because I couldn't be sure they wouldn't have posted a guard on the off-side of the train. I unfastened the gate on the left side of the wagon, peeked out at the night and the empty southbound track, and lowered myself slowly onto a sleeper. I reached up to close the gate then scuttled away down the line, stepping only on the sleepers to reduce noise, and when I reached the end of the train I cut across the track and hid in the undergrowth at the side of the line. Thanks to the slight curvature of the track I had a perfect view of what was going on.

A gang of workers dressed in dark boilersuits had started unloading the wagons. They passed the corpses over their heads in a human chain. In a gap in the undergrowth a large works vehicle had backed up as close as it could get to the line. The bodies were tossed into the back of this vehicle. Some had stiffened and slid around on top of others like a load of discarded shop-window dummies; others were still pliable and their arms and legs cracked and bent this way or that as more were thrown on the pile.

The men emptied at least a dozen wagons and I guessed there must have been at least twenty-five bodies in my own cattle truck. When the first works vehicle could carry no more it drove off down the slope and another took its place. I watched the first vehicle as it rumbled down over the rough ground towards the gasholders. It stopped by a cluster of small outbuildings and another team of workers emerged from the darkness to unload the cargo. Behind the outbuildings were several pipes leading up to the half-empty gasholder. I watched disbelieving as the bodies were carried one at a time and inserted into the broadest of these pipes. It was a slow process: after seven or eight bodies had been tipped into the pipe, the workers could push them no further along inside and they stopped, replaced a cover over the gap in the pipe and opened up a faucet several yards up the pipe. After a few seconds the faucet was closed again and the cover taken off the gap and more corpses stuffed in.

When they had finished, the gasholder seemed to have risen very slightly, but it was almost impossible to tell. There would be room for hundreds of thousands of bodies so it was unlikely a few hundred would make much of an impression.

The teams of men strolled back up the slope in an almost leisurely way and got back on the train, which started moving straight away, back the way it had come, the locomotive pushing from behind.

I crouched down even further in the bushes and watched as the train passed over my head. In the last wagon I saw a group of the corpse carriers. They'd left the truck gate open and were smoking cigarettes, the ends glowing like fireflies as the men stared out into the rushing night. One took a final pull and cast his hot coal into space. It arced through the velvet darkness and landed in the vegetation an inch or two from my face. I held my breath, waiting for the sound of the driver slamming on his brakes, but it didn't come.

BECAUSE I REASONED there was nothing to be gained from a closer inspection of the gasholder or its feeder pipe – and because I was too fucking freaked out to go near it – I crossed the line and fought my way through a set of allotments to get to a road where I flagged down the first minicab I saw and asked the driver to take me into Birmingham.

I was exhausted and my instinct was to go home and collapse, but I was worried about Annie Risk, so I caught the first train from New Street to Manchester. There wasn't time to ring before it left. On the train I fell asleep. If I dreamed at all I woke up when the train braked at a red light outside Piccadilly with no recollection of having done so. I stared out of the window and saw the two giant gasholders over beyond Ancoats. I shivered and pulled my jacket around me. My clothes had dried out after my dip in the canal but I had not warmed up.

I walked down the Piccadilly ramp and crossed the tramlines, having decided to walk to Annie's so I had a chance to get my head together. It wasn't that far, a couple of miles. Within minutes I was marching past the sprawling university buildings. It was late and the streets were deserted. I took in my surroundings, relieved to be back in the real world. Even the wind on my face felt different, slightly cooler than in the City. I plunged into the grid of terraced streets and back entries that was Moss Side.

I stood outside Annie's place for half a minute looking up at her window for signs of life. The light was on but there were no shadows of movement. Pushing open the street door I felt my way through the gloom of the hallway to the stairs and began to climb. My legs felt heavy. At the top I hesitated outside Annie's door and listened again. Nothing. I knocked and waited. There was no sound of activity from within so I knocked again, louder. Still nothing. I tried the handle. The door swung open.

'Annie,' I said quietly as I walked into her flat. 'Annie, are you there?'

The bathroom on my right was in darkness. I checked it nevertheless. It was empty. The little flints of mirrored glass on the wall flickered in the light from the hall. The kitchen was also empty, dirty mugs left standing on the draining board and take-away boxes sticking out of the top of the bin. The light I'd seen from outside was burning in the bedroom, but Annie wasn't there either. The bed was unmade. I glanced in the living room. Empty. I stepped back into the hall then straight back into the living room, my heart in my mouth: I'd glimpsed something on the living room wall and only assimilated it unconsciously.

On the wall in two-foot-high letters – in red – were the crudely daubed words KING KILLER.

I looked in the empty bedroom again. The unmade bed. The light.

My breathing became quick and shallow. Where was Annie Risk?

Chapter Fifteen

IT WAS TOO late to get a train anywhere and when I sat down on Annie's bed to think about what I could do to find her I must have given in to exhaustion because the next thing I knew I was waking up. Light was streaming in at the window. I felt a momentary elation that I was back and then I remembered that Annie was missing. I got up and looked in the other room: I had not dreamt the message on the wall. The red seemed a little less vivid in daylight. Or maybe it was just that it was six hours later and no longer fresh. It had acquired the rusty look of dried blood.

I showered, shaved and dressed in ten minutes, and left the flat.

On my way to Piccadilly I bought a bap, a pack of Camels and a newspaper, which told me it was a Wednesday. So what? On the train I soon put it down unread: I couldn't concentrate on this world while Annie was being held hostage for me in another. The Camels, however, tasted good after the stale muck available in the City.

Arriving in London I went straight to the shop. I pushed the door open against a wodge of circulars, free newspapers and bills. I trailed my finger through a layer of dust on the counter, thought about sticking a record on the turntable and decided against it, in case it turned out to be the recording of my court case. I sat in the back room for a while with a cup of instant coffee and a couple of cigarettes, then went up the back stairs to use the toilet. I sat there looking at the picture of a figure skater in the Winter Olympics I'd clipped from one of the Sunday supplements and tacked to the inside of the door. About to go into a spin, she had already started to turn and twirl her star-speckled black skirt.

I walked downstairs, lit another Camel, stuffed the pack down the side of my left boot and left the shop by the back door.

I found myself stepping directly into a back entry in the City. The air was thicker, warmer on my shaved cheeks. I walked with confidence now I had some purpose other than my own salvation. Soon I was among the crowds. People streamed out of an official-looking building carrying brown paper parcels stencilled with the letter W. I guessed – or understood, as you do in a dream – that W stood for Wednesday, as M had stood for Monday; today's news on the hunt for the escaped King killer. Twenty yards further on was a street-corner judge. I approached him.

'I want to hand myself in,' I said. 'It's me you're looking for. I killed the king.'

He became flustered, calling excitedly for the police. I felt sorry for him. His big chance and he was making a muck of it.

A crowd gathered around us, backing off when they realised what was going on. There was no abuse this time, no angry recriminations, maybe because they hadn't yet had the chance to go home and read their information packs and shoot up whatever drugs the City fed them. It took about three minutes for the police to turn up. I was pushed roughly into the back of a van and driven away. One officer sat in the back with me, restraining a dog. When the van turned a corner, we all lurched in one direction. Eventually the driver braked sharply, I heard footsteps and then the doors were flung open. The dog chased me out into the midday brightness. I blinked, rubbed my eyes.

'Where is she?' I demanded. 'I'm not going anywhere until you tell me where she is.'

Ignoring me, one of the guards grabbed me by the arm and led me through a large open doorway. We walked down a long, green-tiled corridor, my guard's heels snatching metallically at the paved floor. He pushed me to the left through a set of double doors and I stumbled into a reception area. Trophy cabinets stood empty in the middle of the floor. I smelt disinfectant and other institutional smells that made me think of hospitals. A group of people stood waiting for me. Their buckles and buttons gleamed in the harsh light of a single fluorescent strip. A small figure ran out of the centre of the group towards me. The guard let go of me, I opened my arms and Annie Risk bowled headlong into me, almost knocking me over.

They allowed us a few moments. The smell of her hair was instantly familiar despite the fact I'd known her for such a short time. She looked up and I wiped her tears away. And then mine.

'Carl,' she said. 'Carl, Carl.'

'Don't cry, Annie,' I said.

'Carl, you're sick. You've got to get better,' she said, brushing her lovely long black hair out of her eyes. 'All this running around...' she said. 'You've got to get better.'

'Yes, Annie,' I said, not letting her see my confusion. 'I'll be fine. Don't worry about it. I'm feeling better already.'

Had they drugged her? Brainwashed her? Perhaps it wasn't the end of the world. Better she didn't know what was about to happen.

'You've got to go back now, Annie. You can go back. Go back and wait for me.'

I had to tell her something. Over the top of her head I could see the belted-and-buckled advancing towards me as a group.

'You have to let her go,' I said. 'That's the deal.'

They nodded as one man, still moving forward but slowing down and suddenly looking all fuzzy and colour-saturated like a weird music video. They took Annie from me and propelled her towards the door I'd come in by.

'Where are you taking her?' I asked.

'She's going back,' one man confided into my ear as the door to the corridor was pulled open and Annie stepped out. I ran to the door to watch her go. Already she was impossibly far away, vanishing in the distorted perspectives of the green corridor. I felt a hand on my shoulder pulling me back into the bare room.

'It's time,' said a man in a white coat who wasn't White Coat, and suddenly I thought the execution was going to take place in a small private room, perhaps a lethal injection administered by this man. But the buckles and buttons in the large group took control of me and ushered me out into a tunnel. My own footsteps and those of the group behind me echoed around the walls and ceiling. My heart was pumping faster and faster, my mouth drying up like a rose in the desert.

The tunnel sloped upwards and natural light leaked into it from somewhere ahead. The footsteps behind me seemed to speed up, forcing me to do the same and, before I realised fully what was happening, they had faded away while I carried on to the end of the tunnel, where I emerged out onto the pitch. The gates were locked behind me.

It was a big old-fashioned ground with seating areas and terraces. Every available place was occupied. As I walked, blinking in the bright light, into the middle of the vast pitch, the hush that had fallen at my appearance became a murmur that soon grew to a roar of deafening volume. Those who were sitting rose to their feet, tens of thousands of them, wronged citizens, they believed, whose King had been assassinated in cold blood by this bizarre-looking individual now brought to face justice before them.

What would happen to their City once the execution was over? A city whose raison d'être seemed to be the relentless search for their ruler's assassin.

In an instant the crowd fell silent and my ears picked up the insistent rushing beat of a beast's paws upon close-cut grass like a drum roll. I even knew exactly what drum roll it was. The opening bars of 'Shave Your Head'.

I turned around and looked straight into the starved dog's eyes as it sprang at my throat.

But the animal twisted in the air, caught by a single bullet whose report I heard a split second later as it reverberated around the stands. I stared uncomprehendingly at the felled executioner, a single smoking hole torn in the side of its mottled skull. My death had been snatched away from me.

An announcement was made over the PA but it boomed too broadly for my spinning head and the muscles and bones in my legs turned to black night and stars and I collapsed, an approving roar from the crowd battering me finally senseless.

Chapter Sixteen

'YOU WERE AWAY a long time, Carl,' Annie said, taking my hand as we skipped down the last of the steps out of the ground. Behind us the Maine Road faithful could still be heard celebrating City's eighth win in a row. From the Kippax they gave full voice to time-honoured Blues songs and jeered the visiting fans filing out dejectedly from the North Stand.

'I know,' I said, relishing the taste of the November night air, a tang of gunpowder mingling with the petrol fumes and hot dog clouds. It was all *real*.

We walked beneath the mist-shrouded orange lamps of Moss Side's grid of streets, linking arms and talking quietly. I glanced down back entries and Annie reassured me each time something seemed to shift in the shadows.

'There's nothing there,' she'd say, or, 'It's just a dog.'

Just a dog.

We headed towards Rusholme, our goal a relaxing beer and curry. On Great Southern Street a police van crawled along in the traffic snarl-up and I tensed when barking erupted from the back of the van.

'It's all right,' Annie said, putting her arm around my back.

The van rocked from side to side. As we overtook it I looked in at the policemen in the front. They looked complacent, unconcerned about the restless dogs. I shuddered as I pictured the carnage that would be inevitable if the doors were to spring open.

'We're quite safe,' Annie said. 'They're on our side.'

'They don't look like it,' I said, eyeing the officer in the passenger seat, the way he ran his nail-bitten finger over his lip.

I hadn't been as lucky on the motorway as I'd thought I'd been. I never saw my car after the crash, but apparently it looked less like a motor vehicle than an abstract sculpture. Although I had only broken a few minor bones, I lost a lot of blood from lacerations in my neck and side. There had been a dog in the car that hit mine from behind and somehow as our two cars meshed together and cartwheeled across the three lanes the dog had become entangled with me. The shock of the impact and the ordeal I went through waiting for assistance and being cut out of the wreckage took its toll in other ways. As Annie said, I was away for a long time. In a coma, thanks to a substantial blow on the head.

In another place, as *I* explained.

When I finally came back after more than two months, apparently I was babbling, wanting to know what had happened, why they'd shot the dog, why hadn't they let it tear me to pieces? I'd prepared myself for the end and they'd offered it to me on a plate before taking it away again.

Annie had come to the hospital as soon as they found her phone number in the back pocket of my jeans and gave her a ring. She had sat by me and talked to me for days on end, forcing herself to remember tiny details of our short time together that might break through the barrier my mind had erected.

'They even got me to try ringing you, talking to you on the phone while someone held the receiver to your ear. We'd spent so little time together and part of it had been on the telephone just talking. The doctors thought it was worth a try.'

'What did you say on the phone?' I asked her.

'I wasn't sure this was such a good idea, but the doctors thought I ought to appeal to you for help, say that I needed you, that it was terribly important.'

'You got through, Annie. You got through.'

She laughed. We could laugh about it now. 'But you never got back to me,' she answered.

By now we were on the Curry Mile and we'd ordered. The waiter brought us a huge jug of Cobra beer and Annie poured two glasses.

'One of the doctors said there was, and I quote, "a fuck of a lot going on" in your head,' she said.

'Or if he didn't, he should have done,' I said. 'I wonder how they knew.' I recalled White Coat and Gledhill in King's Hospital and then the man in the white coat in the hospital-like interior of the football ground. Green tiles, paved corridors.

'They knew. They know these things.'

We grinned and drank more beer.

'Good stuff,' I said, looking at the golden liquid.

'The best,' Annie confirmed.

We were quiet for a moment. In the weeks since I'd been back, we'd talked around the whole thing a great deal and slowly it was making sense, to Annie as well as to me. They said it would take me a while to get back to full strength. Indeed, as far as my mental condition was concerned, I was suffering from frequent anxiety attacks. Whenever I walked under a railway bridge at night and heard a freight train rattle overhead, or crossed a bridge over a canal and happened to look down, I would go weak at the knees and start shaking.

As for finishing *Un Régicide*, that would have to wait.

'You battled long and hard to come out of the coma,' a doctor had said to me, 'so it's no wonder you should still be feeling the repercussions of that struggle.'

I tried to avoid walking through the interlocking streets of Moss Side at night unless Annie was with me: it was a little bit too much like taking a walk through the coils of my brain. A grey area indeed. I had considered selling the shop and moving back to Manchester. Annie was happy to look after me until I felt myself again, she said. But after a week or two, I realised I needed to know my flat and the shop were there to go back to when I was ready. Consequently, I planned and looked forward to a grand reopening perhaps in a few weeks' time.

'Let's drink to your mother,' Annie said, raising her glass.

'Too right,' I agreed. 'To Mum.'

Without her I might still have been stuck in the City. My mother's spirit had broken after my father's suicide and she had spent many years in hospital, emerging only when the government's Care in the Community programme kicked her out to fend for herself. She went to live in a sheltered housing project and hardly spoke a word to anyone. When Annie went to her and explained how badly I needed her help, some door must have opened in her mind and she agreed to come. She had never harboured any ill will towards me but equally was oblivious to any emotional damage I might have sustained as a result of the suicide.

She had come and sat and talked to me – Annie Risk on one side of the bed, my mother on the other – and that had done the trick.

Later I unscrambled the sense of that final stadium PA announcement in my head. Something about the Queen emerging from exile to issue a pardon. My life had been spared, my guilt rubbed out.

'To you,' I said, lifting my glass to Annie. 'If you hadn't gone to see my mother I wouldn't be here tonight.'

We both drank, I lit a cigarette and at that point, naturally, the food arrived.

I WENT DOWN to see Jaz for the first time since coming out of hospital. I didn't drive, because I didn't have a car any more. You could have offered me a Mini Cooper S, a Mark II Jaguar or a Jensen Interceptor and I still wouldn't have driven. I'd done enough driving for a while.

I went on the train.

I glanced up every branch line that veered off into the trees. I knew where they led now. I sat back, feeling more relaxed than at any point since I'd come out. Gradually my life was getting back to normal. I reached into my left boot for my cigarettes and took one out, lit it and inhaled deeply.

Arriving at Euston I thought about taking a short ride up to the Caledonian Road and having a look at the shop, but decided to go straight to Jaz's place in Bethnal Green. I went south on the Northern Line and headed out east on the Central. I'd cleaned my jacket as best I could. In the crash it had got covered in engine oil and blood, both mine and the dog's. My hair, which they'd shaved so they could open my skull, was growing back. It would take many months before it got to my preferred length, but I could wait.

I walked through the damp, blowy streets of Bethnal Green, crossing the road to avoid the requisite stray dogs in the council block car-park, and enjoyed the solid feel of my boot heels on the stairs up to Jaz's flat. It smelt as glorious as ever.

'It's open,' I heard Jaz shout from some distance as I knocked on his door. I pushed it open and wandered inside. 'Won't be a minute,' he called. 'Just finishing up in here.'

He was in the darkroom.

'I'll get a beer,' I said. 'Do you want one?'

'Yeah,' he shouted. 'In the fridge.'

I looked in the kitchen. He had some strange-looking Thai beer in brown bottles in the fridge. I took two, levered off the caps and set one down on the work surface for Jaz. I took a swig and reached for another cigarette, wandering into the main room. My boots went clump, clump on the bare boards. I swallowed another mouthful of Singha beer and approached the wall to have a look at Jaz's photographs. Clearly he was still doing his urban landscapes thing. The first grim picture – they were all monochrome – showed the tatty car-park opposite his building. He'd caught three dogs sniffing each other. The next was a desolate scene down at Rotherhithe. In the background was a half-full gasholder. I looked back at the first picture of the car-park: the two big gasholders on the other side of the canal were just visible over the top of the old building.

In the third photograph I recognised a pair of gasholders at Wood Green.

The beer sloshed uncomfortably in my stomach as I progressed to the fourth picture: an exterior shot of the Tube station at Bromley By Bow; in the background, out-of-focus but deliberately in the frame, a cluster of gasholders. I counted nine. And they were all full.

I felt a bit sick. A chill crawled spider-like up my spine and I shivered.

There were several more pictures hanging on the walls but I couldn't bring myself to examine them. I was looking out of the window at the two copper-coloured gasholders on the other side of the canal. They were both full as well.

I heard footsteps behind me and dropped the bottle. It didn't smash, just rolled on the boards, tipping out beer. I could feel Jaz's breath on the back of my neck.

'Brother,' he said in a thick, insinuating whisper, 'who the fuck did you think dropped the map in the street for you to find in the first place?'

I turned around slowly to face him. He wasn't alone. Annie Risk was standing next to him. And they were holding hands.

I CALLED OUT and opened my eyes. I was lying in Annie's bed, my T-shirt soaked in sweat. The quilt was on the floor and Annie's side of the bed was empty.

The telephone was ringing in the hallway.

'Annie,' I called.

Apart from the strident tone of the ringing telephone, the flat was silent.

I crawled out of bed, tearing my T-shirt off over my head. I grabbed Annie's bathrobe and went to answer the phone.

'Hello?' I said. 'Hello?'

There was no one there. Just the barely perceptible metallic scrape of a missed connection.

I hung up.

I shivered and pulled the bath robe tighter around my shoulders.

And then came the knock on the door.

Acknowledgements

The author would like to thank Kate Ryan, Florence Secret Rousselle, Jonathan Rees, Sarah Llewellyn-Jones, Chloë Bryan-Brown, Bill Starling (formerly of British Gas), Ian Cunningham.

Thanks to Paul J McAuley and Kim Newman, who published the short story 'Night Shift Sister', which formed the basis of this novel, in their anthology 'In Dreams' (Victor Gollancz).

Special thanks to all former members of the Passage, especially Richard Witts, Andy Wilson and Joe McKechnie. And to James Nice of LTM, who made the Passage back catalogue available on CD.